MOONLIGHT
& LOVE SONGS

ALYSSA LINN PALMER

Have you purchased the paperback and wish you had a copy

for your e-reader? E-mail the author for details.

ISBN: 099200652X
ISBN-13: 978-0992006525

The door opened and a man stumbled in, long and lean, in dark jeans, a slightly battered leather jacket and a grey scarf slung haphazardly around his neck. His dark blond hair had been slicked back but it fell over his forehead as he dropped a duffel bag that had seen better years at his feet. He looked exhausted, dark hollows under his eyes and a paleness that seemed more than just skin color.

Alain looked him over and he and Benoît exchanged glances. The man gave his bag a kick, pushing it against the bar.

"Drink?" he said, raising his eyebrows. His eyes were a bright blue, or at least, Benoît imagined they might be, if there was a sudden burst of sunlight to illuminate the man's sculptured face. His cheekbones were high, but not too high, and his nose seemed just a bit too big for his face, in a charming way, but the slow smile that spread over his lips made Benoît want to kiss him right then and there. Thin but not sparse, they looked just right to soften under pressure but give back as good as they got.

Benoît pushed the empty snifter back to Alain. If he didn't get a grip, he'd lose any chance of finishing out the night without stumbling through 'La Vie En Rose'. Those lips would have to be someone else's.

THE LE CHAT ROUGE SERIES

DEDICATION

To Jon—thank you for everything,
for being my uncle, but also for being
my friend. Love you lots.

CONTENTS

ACKNOWLEDGMENTS

Thank you to Cathy Pegau, my friend and one of my first readers for this story. Your feedback has been essential. Thank you to Jon, for being one of my first readers, and for being willing to brainstorm and discuss drugs and sex over bowls of Vietnamese food. Thank you to Elizabeth Otto, EMT, for her knowledge and her willingness to answer questions on drug overdoses. And thank you, as always, to my family, and the Calgary RWA for their support.

CHAPTER 1

There was nothing sadder than an empty club.

Benoît liked to think Le Chat Rouge was quiet because it was Tuesday, but Sera wasn't there to charm the clientele anymore. The strains of '*Stardust*' from his piano echoed through the barren club. It was early yet—even Patrice and Serge, his bandmates, had yet to arrive. Jean, the maître'd and the owner's right-hand man, would be furious.

They needed a singer. He didn't even care who, as long as they wouldn't skip out after a night or two, as every new hire had done since Sera left. Trouble was, once they had a taste of this rundown jazz bar, they were off to greener pastures. He'd considered it himself, but, comfortable in his position, he delayed. Among the drunks, the worn velvet banquettes, the creaking parquet floors and the tiny dressing rooms, it felt like home. And where would he go? He'd left his old life in Clamecy behind as soon as he'd finished his schooling, eager to sample the cosmopolitan capital. Of course, if he'd known he'd end up here, he might not have been so eager.

The door opened, spilling a hint of weak sunlight across the floor, but it was only Patrice and Serge. Benoît kept playing, his hands wandering the keys, riffing off the popular tune into something all his own.

Jean emerged from the back corridor with an empty brandy snifter and dirty dishes, and he threw Benoît a cool look. Handing off the dishes to Alain, the bartender, a slim young man with perfectly arranged dark hair, he came down the three steps to stand in front of the stage, scowling at Benoît. The intimidating effect was nullified from Benoît's current position, a foot or two above Jean. He segued into another Hoagy Carmichael tune, playing it with no deviations, but Jean still scowled.

"Patrice! Serge!"

Patrice halted in the tuning of his cello, but Serge tapped the high hat, looking unconcerned at Jean's bellowing.

"Did you have a request?" Benoît drawled in English, like he'd do for any tourist.

"Shut it," Jean said and Benoît shrugged. "This is the third time you've both been late. If it happens again, you're through."

Patrice protested but Serge merely gave Jean a dark look.

"And then what?" Benoît asked. "We've already lost our last singer—pretty soon you'll have no one left. Then who will buy the drinks and pay our wages?"

"There's a new singer coming in from Marseille on tonight's train," Jean said.

"Is she good?"

"He," and Jean emphasized the word, "is one of the best." He straightened his waistcoat. "And if he quits, I'll make sure all three of you are out of work. More dedicated musicians would be drawing in the crowds." He gave them a final stern look before he strode back to the bar.

"This guy better be good," Patrice said.

"Not like the last one—she couldn't sing her way out of a bucket," Serge replied.

"He can't be any worse," Benoît said.

Patrice leaned forward, his hand out. Benoît passed him the setlist. "Is that all?"

"If we don't close down early tonight, we'll do a short set of Piaf songs," Benoît said. "But I doubt we'll need it."

An older couple walked into the club, their steps hesitant when they saw they were the only customers. Jean greeted them with an obsequious smile before they could retreat, and they reluctantly followed him to a table near the stage. Benoît acknowledged them with a nod and a smile far more genuine than Jean's had been. The woman returned his smile and her husband appeared to relax back into his seat. They had a whispered conference and then the woman rose and came towards the stage, smoothing her linen skirt. Benoît let the song taper off.

"Can you play 'As Time Goes By'?" she asked. "It's one of my favourites." Her French was shaky, and he'd played that song so many times that he had nightmares of becoming an automaton in a gilded music box, but Benoît gave her as much of a bow as he could from his seat at the piano.

"Bien sûr, madame." He nodded to Patrice and Serge, and they began. Her delighted smile made it worthwhile. With luck, they'd tip before they left.

When the band finished her requested song, they continued with a medley that Benoît had developed especially for the Casablanca requests. It kept the audience from requesting '*As Time Goes By*' multiple times, and it earned them decent tips. He didn't mind those sorts of tourists.

A few more couples trickled in, but the night was quieter than most. By ten-thirty, the club was nearly empty again and Benoît let the music fade out. Serge and Patrice took over with a composition they'd been working on and Benoît headed over to the bar, stretching out his back and hearing the pop of his spine. Alain poured him a brandy, the cheap stuff, but he wasn't complaining, and slid it across the bar.

"That American couple sang your praises to Jean," Alain said.

"That'll keep him off my back," Benoît replied, taking a deep gulp of the brandy. It burned in his throat, but the alcohol gave him a little boost. He rubbed his eyes and leaned over to look in the mirror behind the bar, pushing a hand through his curly dark hair. Another hour and he'd be done. Not that going back to his tiny and sparse studio flat was anything to get excited about. The advert had said 'cosy', if a single room with a kitchen and a wet-room bathroom with shower was cosy. Considering what he spent on rent, he considered another c-word: criminal. But it was a place to rest.

Benoît tossed back the rest of his brandy, then straightened his bow tie before smoothing down his jacket. He'd rather play in jeans and shirtsleeves, but Jean would have a fit. And the owner, Monsieur Royale, would probably lumber out of his office to give Benoît the sack personally. Wouldn't that be a sight to see.

The door opened and a man stumbled in, long and lean, in dark jeans, a slightly battered leather jacket and a grey scarf slung haphazardly around his neck. His dark blond hair had been slicked back but it fell over his forehead as he dropped a duffel bag that had seen better years at his feet. He looked exhausted, dark hollows under his eyes and a paleness that seemed more than just skin color.

Alain looked him over and he and Benoît exchanged glances. The man gave his bag a kick, pushing it against the bar.

"Drink?" he said, raising his eyebrows. His eyes were a bright blue, or at least, Benoît imagined they might be, if there was a sudden burst of sunlight to illuminate the man's sculptured face. His cheekbones were high, but not too high, and his nose seemed just a bit too big for his face, in a charming way, but the slow smile that spread over his lips made Benoît want to kiss him right then and there. Thin but not sparse, they looked just right to soften under pressure but give back as good as they got. Those lips reminded him of Nicolas, the last man he'd dated, the one he'd found sucking another man's cock in the toilets here at the club. They hadn't dated long, but it had been long enough. Long enough to remind him exactly why he shouldn't bother. His father had told him he'd strayed from what was proper, and it was his own fault. He deserved to be alone. Whether or not his father had been right, life agreed with the old man. And he didn't need to be tempting fate, not with this man. He'd be miserable once again, and that was the way things worked.

Benoît threw another glance towards the man as he pushed the empty snifter back to Alain. Beautiful, and tempting. If he didn't get a grip, he'd lose any chance of finishing out the night without stumbling through '*La Vie En Rose*'. Those lips would have to be someone else's. He was meant to take on life alone. He turned to head back to the stage and tripped over the duffel bag. The man caught him by the arm, and the touch felt like electricity. He caught his breath. The man seemed to catch his own breath, and Benoît knew he hadn't been the only one to feel it. Who was he? He heard Patrice and Serge finishing their song, and knew he had to get back to the stage, but he wanted to know more, to talk to this man.

Benoît steadied himself and the man let go, though their gazes still held. The moment lengthened and was broken by Jean, who came up to the bar and barked orders at Alain before turning his glare on Benoît. Benoît gave the man a look he hoped was apologetic and headed back to the stage. Patrice and Serge exited stage left, going into the dressing room. Their evening was done, and now it was his turn to finish the night. A few more classics for the stalwart occupants of the club, and then it would be over.

The man at the bar turned to watch and Benoît gave a little extra flourish to his movements. Sera would have teased him and called it flirting, but he wasn't, not really. He didn't need to take this man back to his cosy flat. That would create complications, even if they were short-lived. He knew his taste in men was poor. He only ever fell for the ones that were bad news, and he'd just avoid this one. But later, under the hot water, he'd jerk off to thoughts of those lips, those blue eyes, his strong hand.

Benoît looked down at the keys and when he looked up again, the man had disappeared. He felt a pang of disappointment.

Feelings like that led to nothing good. It was probably best that the man left without saying goodbye.

He finished off the set with a slow rendition of Hoagy Carmichael's '*How Little We Know*'. Without a singer, it felt flat, stripped of its flirty connotations. He drew out the last few notes, then pushed back from the piano. Time to go home.

He stopped by the bar on the way out to say goodnight to Alain, who was putting away the booze and wiping down the stainless steel counter.

"Sounds like you'll have company tomorrow night," Alain said.

"The singer?"

Alain indicated the back hallway. "He's in there now with Jean and Royale, probably hashing out terms."

"I didn't see him come in."

Alain gave him an incredulous look. "You tripped over him, you idiot."

"Him?" Benoît could hardly believe his luck. Fate, it seems, had plans.

"Daniel."

Benoît woke late in the afternoon. At first he couldn't remember why he felt such anticipation, but then it came to him. Tonight there would be Daniel. He hurried into the shower, tapping his feet on the tile in time with the music in his head. Afterwards, he dressed in his spare suit, folding up the one he'd worn the night before and tossing it into a carrier bag. He'd drop it at a dry-cleaners on his way to work. His stomach growled as he passed a crêpe stand on the rue Saint-Denis and he doubled back and joined the queue.

He felt like a kid, full of nervous energy, and he shifted from foot to foot, causing the woman in line behind him to clear her throat. When he glanced back, she gave him an annoyed look.

"Pardon, madame," he said, but a minute later, he was back at it.

When he had his crêpe—a savory galette filled with meat and cheese, he devoured it as he walked, finishing it before he crossed the Seine and headed towards Le Chat Rouge. He crumpled the wrapper in his hand, and once he entered the club, he tossed it at Edouard, the evening's bartender.

"Salut!"

Edouard tossed the ball back and they batted it back and forth until Jean arrived. Edouard snatched the ball out of the air and gave Jean a sheepish look.

"Daniel will be here shortly for you to rehearse," Jean said. "Treat him well, Benoît, or I'll find another pianist."

Benoît spread his arms. "What do you take me for?"

"We've had four singers through here since Mademoiselle Durand left."

"That's hardly my fault," Benoît replied. It was mostly true.

The first singer after Sera sang flat, and a few choice words sent her packing. Jean would have done the same, if he'd stopped staring at the woman's ample chest.

The others had been less remarkable, staying only long enough to hear the siren song of nicer, better-paying clubs, but he didn't say as much to Jean.

"Does he prefer Louis Armstrong or Frank Sinatra?" Benoît asked instead.

"He's skilled at all the classic songs," Jean said as if it should be obvious.

"Where did you find him?"

"He came recommended by one of Monsieur Royale's contacts," Jean replied.

Then he must be brilliant, Benoît thought. He wouldn't dare openly disparage the tastes of one of Royale's friends. "I'll be waiting," he said.

Jean paced back into the corridor, no doubt going to count the liquor again. Edouard chuckled to himself. "So, who is this paragon?"

"Daniel something-or-other," Benoît replied. "I only saw him briefly last night. I hope he really can sing."

"We were spoiled with Sera here," Edouard said.

"We were. Have you heard from her, or has Sophie?"

"Sophie did last week." Edouard became a bit dreamy-eyed. Young love. A shame Edouard was straight—his olive complexion and dark eyes were charming. He and Sophie were almost inseparable. "Sera and Marc were in London."

"I thought she had family in Marseille."

"Maybe that's all settled. But they're in London for now. Happy, I guess."

"Good." After all her trouble, Sera deserved some happiness. "And how are things with your ladylove?" Benoît couldn't not ask. Edouard would tell him anyway.

"I can't remember what it was like without her," Edouard replied. "But she has to apply for residency, and I don't know how that will go." He looked pensive as he straightened the bottles behind the bar.

"It'll work out."

"I hope so."

Before he headed to the dressing room, Benoît gave Edouard what he hoped was a reassuring smile. Sometimes he envied Edouard his happiness, but mostly he just observed from a distance. Easier that way. But with Daniel…

Glancing into the dressing room's clouded mirror, he straightened his suit and pulled a bow tie from his pocket, leaning forward as he put it on. Maybe that frisson he felt with Daniel was a one-time thing, a reaction to a new face. By tonight he'd be immune and better for it. The temptation would be gone. There was a knock on the door and it opened. Daniel stood there, and Benoît felt his heart skip a beat. No, not a one-time thing.

The man was ready for a performance, dressed in a pristine tailored black suit, with a shirt so white and crisp it hardly seemed real. Unlike Benoît, Daniel's tie hung around his neck, much like his scarf had the night before. It suited him, made him seem rakish, debonair. He'd have the ladies eating out of his hand. Benoît's heart sank. Lucky ladies.

"Jean said I'd find you here. I'm Daniel Marceau."

"Benoît Grenier." He held out his hand, and Daniel took it. The frisson between them startled him. It hadn't just been a one-off. He sucked in a breath.

"What's the setlist for tonight?" Daniel asked, edging into the small room. He seemed to be unaffected by their proximity. The walls shrank in on themselves until Benoît could focus on nothing else but Daniel. He wore an understated scent, masculine and simple, and Benoît found himself inhaling deeply. He caught himself, and stiffened his spine.

"Jean didn't give you any details?" His question came out sharply, and he had to keep himself from grimacing.

"Nothing, except that he was glad I was a man, so I wouldn't be singing any Dietrich. Then he muttered something about the Boche."

"His father was in the war. Sera used to put Dietrich into the setlists just to provoke him." Benoît needed to get some air; Daniel was too close. "Let's go to the piano."

Once he'd settled on the bench and lifted the fallboard, Benoît gestured to Daniel. The man stood facing him, resting an elbow on the polished dark wood.

"With the chanteuses, the sets had a lot of Piaf," Benoît said, absentmindedly tickling out the opening notes to '*Je ne regrette rien*'. "The tourists love it, of course. When I'm on my own, I'd much rather play some Hoagy Carmichael or Louis Armstrong."

"I'm good with those," Daniel said. "Some of the Piaf, too, though not all."

Benoît fumbled in his pocket and drew out a crumpled setlist. He flipped it over and took his pen from where he'd left it on the keys the night before. "I take requests," he said, looking up at Daniel, his pen tip poised. Daniel leaned closer and Benoît held his breath. Another foot and he could kiss those lips.

Daniel rattled off half a dozen songs and Benoît forced himself to focus, scribbling down the titles.

"And how about '*Baltimore Oriole*' for the last song of the first set?" he suggested. "Classic, American, and just a bit poignant."

"D'accord. And start the new set with something catchy and upbeat, like '*Grands Boulevards*', or perhaps '*Le p'tit mome*', by Montand?"

They worked out the rest of the set, but Benoît paused on the last song. He wanted something impressive, something that would show off both their skills. He tapped the pen on the fallboard.

"We need Piaf," Daniel said. Benoît's hand slipped on the keys and he winced at the discordant notes.

"Sorry." He willed the piano to silence but the sound still echoed in his ears.

"You think I can't sing a Piaf song?" Daniel asked. His tone was suddenly scathing and Benoît couldn't help the flush that rose in his cheeks.

"Which one do you want to do? I've rarely heard Piaf done well." He kept his statement matter-of-fact, though he couldn't bring down the heat of his cheeks.

"'*Je ne regrette rien*', of course," Daniel replied.

Benoît sighed. "It's not that I doubt you," he said, trying to explain his reaction. "I've just heard too many chanteurs butcher the songs."

Daniel relaxed a fraction, his slim fingers worrying the corner of the setlist. His nails were well-kept and manicured, but the back of his hand seemed speckled with little white scars. How strange.

Daniel took up the pen and scrawled the song title at the bottom of their list.

"Want to try one out before Serge and Patrice get here?" Benoît started in on Louis Armstrong's '*What a Wonderful World*'.

Daniel grimaced. "That one?"

"It's my most common request, aside from the Casablanca tunes. Now that you're here, I'd put money on it that you'll be singing it every night."

Daniel groaned, a low sound that Benoît wanted to hear

again under different circumstances. Daniel stepped to the microphone and took it from its stand, returning to stand by the piano facing Benoît. "Commencez, monsieur."

CHAPTER 2

Back in the confines of his tiny room, Daniel shed his tuxedo jacket and hung it up, carefully smoothing out the wrinkles. He did the same with his trousers and shirt, then fell back onto the chilled duvet. The light from the moon shone into the dirty gable window and he reached over to pull the dusty curtain across, letting loose a sneeze. The light of the single lamp made the place look nicer than it was, but he'd lived in worse.

Hell, he'd left behind worse than this. His room in Marseille had been large and sumptuous, but the furnishings hadn't mattered. There'd been girls, and boys, a new one every night. And the drugs. He rubbed his hands together, then up over his arms, feeling the scars from the track marks.

Here was better, even if the room was the size of a closet. He hadn't expected Royale to put him up in a palace, but this tiny room a few floors above Le Chat Rouge was hardly big enough for a bed.

He rubbed his arms again, this time from the chill. If only he had just one hit—just one—he could ignore the lack of heat, ignore the room, ignore everything. He rose and pushed back the covers, crawling wearily under the duvet. Better not to think of it. Think of something else.

The piano player. Benoît. He'd always liked musicians, admired their technical skill, their virtuosity. He could sing, but he had only a rudimentary skill with instruments. If he could, he would have watched Benoît all night as he played, charming the audience, his slight smile hinting at the dimple in his cheek.

Benoît could be his audience of one. Desire surged through him at the thought and he felt suddenly warm under the duvet. But it couldn't be. Where lovers were concerned, he knew he couldn't trust his own judgment. He'd never once chose rightly.

Moonlight shimmered through the ragged holes in the curtain and he flopped over in bed, facing away from the window. Closing his eyes, he let his breathing slow, counting each inhalation. It was better than counting sheep, or cracks in the wall. The warmth under the duvet grew and he felt sweat prickle under his arms and behind his knees. He shifted position, lying on his back again, but it didn't help.

Daniel had only been able to sleep well on the train from Marseille. Something about the movement, the sound of the wheels skimming the rails, the murmur of voices. Here it was too quiet, too easy for his mind to fill in the silence, reminding him of his cravings. He squeezed his eyes shut. Think of the music, of Benoît at the piano, playing 'Baltimore Oriole'. Better to have a song stuck in his head. He hummed along to the music.

He could do this. He'd left all the bad stuff back in Marseille. Most of it. He knew Royale's type, knew the deal he'd made, but with his eyes open…

Footsteps thumped on the stairs and the floor in the hall creaked. A door slammed and all was quiet once more. Daniel kept humming, moving onto a Yves Montand song. There was a low moan from the next room, gasping cries. Daniel turned over in bed and pulled the pillow around his ears. The noises continued, growing in pitch until he couldn't ignore them. Was every night going to be like this?

Finally the woman gave a shriek and fell silent. He didn't hear her companion, but after a short break, he heard two sets of footsteps clatter down the hallway. A shiver swept over him. He turned on the lumpy mattress, bringing his knees up to his chest. If he just ignored the craving, it would go away. It had to.

"Where is he?" Jean left his post at the door and strode down to the stage.

Benoît glanced at his watch. They should have started their set ten minutes ago, but Daniel had yet to appear. Maybe he'd decided to skip out. Another bad choice, but if Daniel wasn't here, then things could continue on as they'd been. "I'm not his keeper."

"If he's quit because of you—" Jean threatened.

"He was fine last night. And look." Benoît gestured to the bar. Daniel had appeared, but he looked unkempt, not like the night before. Jean stalked up to the bar and though Benoît couldn't hear every word, he recognized Jean's scolding, furious tone. He thought Daniel might shrink under the onslaught—most did—but instead he seemed to let Jean's words roll over him. Finally Jean let him go and Daniel came up to the stage.

He looked more of a mess close up, though he'd obviously tried to appear at least half-decent. His suit was rumpled, as was his shirt, and his bow tie hung limply. But the worst of it was his face—pale, almost sallow, dark smudges under his eyes. His hair had been slicked back but it wasn't behaving. Hardly the handsome, assured man he'd been last night.

Benoît rose from his place at the piano, feeling some pity. The man looked like he hadn't slept a wink.

"We'll be back," he said to Serge and Patrice. "Keep the masses entertained."

Serge chuckled at that. "D'accord."

"Come with me." Benoît took an unprotesting Daniel by the arm and led him into Sera's old dressing room, now his. "Sit down."

Daniel flopped bonelessly into the chair, raising a puff of dust. Benoît pulled open the top drawer of the vanity, bringing out pots of concealer, foundation and powder. He thanked the god he didn't believe in when the second drawer held application sponges. In a few minutes, Daniel would look human again. He'd had to resort to the same thing himself once or twice. He picked up the pot of foundation and unscrewed the lid.

"Is this really necessary?" Daniel rubbed his eyes.

"You look like shit," Benoît said. No point mincing words. "What did you do all night?" He nudged Daniel's chin, tilting his face up to get a better angle, and began to apply the foundation. Slowly the sallow tinge disappeared under the makeup and the dark circles under Daniel's eyes were greatly reduced. Benoît took up the powder.

"I didn't do anything." Daniel squeezed his eyes shut as Benoît patted his forehead with the powder puff.

"Hard to believe." It needled him, that Daniel had probably been out carousing. Had he picked up a young man—or a young woman? Was that why he was so tired? Too much partying?

Daniel grabbed his wrist and Benoît felt the frisson of electricity. "I know what you're thinking, but I didn't get drunk. I couldn't sleep."

Benoît pulled his hand free. He wouldn't let Daniel affect him. It was just business. "Keep this up and you'll be sacked," he warned. Once he finished with the powder he pinched Daniel's cheeks to bring up a bit of color.

"I need somewhere to sleep," Daniel complained as he stood. Benoît straightened his suit jacket and tried not to think of where Daniel could rest his naked body. He took the bow tie from where it hung around Daniel's neck.

"Where are you staying?" He slipped the tie underneath Daniel's collar, trying to convince himself he'd asked that question just to make conversation. He tied the bow tie carefully, focusing on his fingers, not on Daniel's blue eyes, or his kissable lips. His gaze flicked up. Damn.

"Upstairs. It sounded like a brothel for awhile, then I couldn't get to sleep."

"Jean likes to fuck women up there," Benoît said, "so he doesn't have to go home and fuck his wife." He didn't know if

Jean had a wife; the man didn't seem like the type.

"Do you know somewhere else I could stay? Somewhere cheap?"

In my bed. Benoît bit his tongue. No, he couldn't say it.

"I'll ask around," he said instead, avoiding Daniel's gaze. "Hard to get much that's cheap around here. Let's go."

He bumbled the first song. It was an easy one, '*Mon manège à moi*', and he'd played it a hundred times. But tonight, with thoughts of Daniel, rumpled and sleeping in his bed, he had to repeat the introduction. Jean gave him a hard stare from the bar, but Daniel, for all his exhaustion, was a pro. The clientele didn't seem to notice the slip.

Benoît kept his eyes on the music or the ivory keys, managing to get through the rest of the set without any mistakes. He avoided Daniel at the break, and even Jean, heading past them into the back hallway, past Royale's door and out into the alleyway. The cool air settled him, though it smelled of the rubbish bins a few feet away, a low, sour scent of spoiled food and refuse.

He ran a finger around the inside of his collar. Daniel was just another singer. A fellow professional. He'd be fine.

Benoît returned to the warm, smoky interior of the club. At the bar, Edouard passed him a brandy.

"Don't mind his majesty," Edouard said, his mouth quirking up with amusement. "He's having a bad day."

Benoît glanced over at Jean, who patiently herded a small group of octogenarians to the door, fawning over them. As the maître'd waved off the last elderly man, Benoît hooked his fingers around the glass. "I'd best get back."

"Be quick, he's coming." Edouard went back to work, replacing clean glasses and wiping down his work area.

Benoît strode down to the stage. Serge and Patrice had resumed their spots, but Daniel wasn't there.

"Dressing room." Serge nodded towards the door. Benoît put the brandy on the piano and went over. He didn't even bother to knock, just pushed his way in.

Daniel blotted his forehead with a handkerchief, then his cheeks. He looked pale under the makeup and his eyes were red-rimmed, bloodshot.

"I'm coming," he said without turning, taking up the powder puff resting on the vanity. He powdered his face, masking the slight sheen of perspiration.

"Jean's going to have our heads after tonight."

Daniel glanced over. "We'll be fine." He repeated himself, his voice stronger. "Let's go."

There was a smattering of applause as they mounted the stage. Daniel gave an elegant bow to the audience as he reached the microphone, and Benoît copied him before he sat at the piano. The glass of brandy shimmered in the spotlight and he wished he'd had time to drink it.

"Maestro, if you please." Daniel looked over his shoulder, a slow smile crossing his features. If Benoît didn't know better, he'd think Daniel was flirting with him. "Pour votre plaisir, mesdames et messieurs, '*How Little We Know*'."

Benoît's hands went to the keys. Just think of the music.

CHAPTER 3

He wanted to be in Marseille. He'd call up his dealer and this feeling would go away. Daniel scrubbed his face with a hand. His dealer was the reason he had to leave in the first place. His bosses didn't want the scandal and he still needed a job. Hence this "favour" they'd suggested. He didn't like owing favours to anyone, especially a man like Royale. They always got him into trouble.

Daniel paced his small room, or rather, he took two steps to the door, pivoted on one foot and took three steps back. The slight movement made him more agitated instead of calming him. He needed a walk. No, what he really needed was a fuck, but that wouldn't happen. He'd seen the slight interest from Benoît that evening as the pianist had tried to make him presentable, but it had disappeared as fast as Benoît did at the end of the night.

A walk it was.

He grabbed his leather jacket and put on his shoes, making his way softly down the back stairs. He found the key for the back door, tucked in a drawer behind the bar as Jean had showed him.

"You get locked out, there's no one coming to let you back in," Jean had warned.

He didn't want to walk the streets until dawn. The back door creaked as he opened it and he tested the key, just to be sure, then eased the door closed and stepped out into the grungy, dark alleyway. The smell from the bins faded as he hit the street, a gust of wind chilling him. He did up his jacket and walked out to the boulevard.

Fifteen minutes one way, and fifteen minutes back, he figured. That would do it. He headed north and crossed the Pont Neuf. He tucked his hands into his coat pockets and continued past the dim glow of shops shuttered for the night, slowing to a meandering stroll when he reached the glass arch of Les Halles. A group of young men in hoodies and jeans lingered nearby, the glow of their cigarettes little beacons in the shadow.

One of the boys gave him a once over, then said something to his friends in a language Daniel didn't know. He lingered until one of the other young men sauntered over.

"Can I have a cigarette?" Daniel asked when the boy drew nearer.

"Une cigarette?" the boy asked, sounding skeptical. Then he shrugged and drew out a packet of Marlboro Lights. Daniel grimaced.

"Marlboro rouge?" he asked. The boy shook his head and proffered the pack one more time. Daniel took a cigarette and the boy drew out a lighter. He flicked it once, twice, and then the flame held, illuminating them both. The boy's eyes were dark like his hair, and his skin was olive-toned. Moroccan, perhaps, or

Algerian, he thought. While he smoked the cigarette, they looked each other over, judging their worth.

"What do you need?" the boy asked. Daniel knew what he needed to help him sleep.

"Hashish?" he asked. The boy grinned.

"Money first," he said, gesturing to one of his companions, who came forward warily, his hands in the pockets of his puffy jacket.

Daniel dug into his pocket and pulled out a few small bills. The boy took them and nodded to the other, who produced a bag with two rolled joints.

"Hashish spécial," the boy said as he handed it over. The boys retreated to their group and Daniel tucked the bag into his jacket pocket, feeling some relief. Now he could sleep.

He retraced his path along the rue Pont Neuf and back across to the Left Bank. By the time he reached the alley door of Le Chat Rouge, he was chilled through. He let himself in and replaced the key. In his room, he cracked open the tiny window and took out the first joint. From his duffel bag he took a lighter and lit the hand-rolled marijuana. The smell of tobacco smoke and hash filled the room and he inhaled deeply, gratefully, feeling the tension beginning to fade.

Daniel sat on the bed. The next toke tasted bitter, but the one after that was normal again. Hashish spécial?

By the time he'd smoked almost the entire joint, his head spun and he felt euphoric, a tingling awareness of his body spreading throughout every pore. That hashish wasn't just hashish. He blinked, but the shadows in the room still shimmered in his vision. Rubbing his eyes didn't help. He took a deep breath. He shouldn't have bought those joints, but the feeling…

Daniel stretched out on the bed and kicked off his shoes. He hadn't felt this good in weeks. He began to feel sleepy, his eyes heavy. He didn't even try to fight it.

Every song they played, Daniel was on. He hit every note, every cue, and he had the Saturday night audience clamouring for more. Even Monsieur Royale came out from his office, sitting at his reserved table with a glass of cognac and a cigarette.

At the break, the female contingent of the audience seemed to swarm the stage, mooning over Daniel, who gave them a close-up dose of his charm. Benoît edged through the crowd, heading towards the bar, trying to ignore the sight of Daniel with his arm over the shoulders of a lovely young redheaded woman. She leaned into him, and to Benoît, Daniel looked just as enraptured.

"If he does this every night, I think Royale's financial worries are over," Alain said as he poured Benoît's brandy. Behind him, Edouard readied a bucket with ice and a bottle of champagne for Jean, who waited at the end of the bar.

"If we can get him away from his fan club," Benoît replied, trying to keep the sourness from his tone.

"They'll leave and tell all their friends." Jean looked like the cat who'd eaten the canary. He scooped up the silver bucket and a pair of champagne flutes. "Even Mademoiselle Durand couldn't do that."

Benoît watched as Jean took the champagne over to an older couple. "He's sure smug, like he discovered Daniel himself."

"I heard it was a favour," Alain replied. He poured two glasses of beer while he talked. "Royale said something to Jean about it while I was stocking up for tonight."

Benoît frowned. "What sort of favour?"

"Maybe Royale called one in?" Alain said. "It sucked pretty bad when they couldn't find a good singer after Sera left."

"With talent like that?" Benoît didn't believe it. Daniel had the charisma and skill to be singing on the best stages in Europe.

"Not if he has more off days like he did the other night," Edouard said.

Benoît tossed back his brandy. Time to take Daniel away from all those women. One more set, and an encore, and he could have a few more drinks.

He wove through the women still around Daniel and clapped him on the shoulder. It was like touching a live wire, and they both felt it.

"Break's over, ladies," Daniel said genially, disentangling himself from the redhead's grasp. She'd been the most persistent, even though more than a few women had come to speak to him.

"I didn't know you had such a fan club," Benoît said as they mounted the stairs to the stage. "Did they follow you from Marseille?"

"I hope not." Daniel grimaced and pushed away the lock of hair that had fallen over his forehead. Benoît was puzzled. Surely Daniel would be happy to see fans from home?

"Let's start with something more romantic," Daniel said. Benoît tickled the keys, playing the first few chords of '*La Vie En Rose*'. "Perfect. We'll knock 'em dead."

After they'd finished the encore, with a crowd-rousing rendition of '*Jezebel*', Daniel brushed off the women who'd fawned over him at the break. He'd had enough. Instead, he followed Benoît as he left the club, catching him by the arm.

"Want to go for a drink?" he suggested. Benoît's usually bored expression slid away, replaced by a slow, sensual smile, showing the dimple on his cheek. A feeling he'd experienced only from drugs began to coalesce inside him. Excitement. That smile did something to him.

"I know just the place," Benoît said.

They headed down the boulevard, away from the busier tourist areas and into a small side street. A tiny café, its neon lights sputtering, sat open, half full of late night bar-goers. Young lovers were ensconced in a back booth, more interested in each other than their coffees going cold on the table. A grizzled man wrapped his aged hands around a white porcelain cup, his shoulders hunched. A loud group of youths crowded a trio of tables near the front.

The middle-aged man behind the counter, his waistcoat rumpled and his tie crooked, gave them a welcoming smile. "Benoît, good to see you. It's been awhile."

"Gregoire." Benoît shook the man's hand. "I'll have my usual." He glanced over, and Daniel hesitated.

"Whiskey," he said finally. It would keep him from lying awake the rest of the night, as much as he'd rather have a café crème, like the young lovers. When he dug into his pocket to pay, Benoît stilled his hand.

"Allow me," he said, his voice huskier than usual. He dropped Daniel's hand, and Daniel missed the warmth.

"I'll get the next one," he said, which provoked a smile from Benoît.

"This one's to celebrate your arrival," Benoît said. "Before you came, I had to sit through a bunch of amateurs."

Gregoire returned with their drinks, but Daniel fidgeted at the implied praise. He loved to sing, loved that feeling when he was giving his all, and seeing the crowd respond, but he knew he could do so much better.

"I'm an amateur," he said once they'd seated themselves at an empty table.

"Neither of us are amateurs," Benoît replied. "Where were you before here? How did Royale find you?"

"I've played at lots of clubs," he said, being purposefully vague. He didn't want to say. It was too easy to check his facts, to find out the truth. "It wasn't working out. I needed somewhere solid, reliable." It was a good line, but it was Le Chat Rouge or nothing. He was determined to make this work, if he could just get through the insomnia, the need that pricked him when he least wanted it.

"Infighting?" Benoît asked. "The club I started out at—it's closed now—always had bickering between the musicians. Here, we just have Jean, the common enemy." He gave Daniel a wry smile and sipped his brandy.

"Not exactly." Daniel didn't want to talk about himself any further. His arms prickled and he thought of the nights he'd spent, the post-performance parties…Dionysian worship at its worst. But it had seemed so fun, so glamourous. At first.

"Trouble?" Benoît gave him a look, more perceptive than Daniel had expected.

"I don't want to talk about it." Daniel took a gulp of his whiskey and Benoît sat back, his fingers curling around the stem of his brandy glass. It wasn't just the drugs, but what happened while he was on them. Royale's words came back to him.

"Do as you're told, and you'll do well here," he'd said, looking at Daniel meaningfully. "You know what will happen if I send you back."

Back. Back to the drugs, and to the pushers who thought he'd sold them out to the cops.

Benoît leaned forward, running his finger down the back of Daniel's hand, over the pale needle scars. Daniel flinched, but Benoît didn't seem to notice the marks.

"You're the best singer I've worked with," Benoît said. He seemed to be considering something. "If we struck out on our own, we could tour France. Make some money."

Where had that come from?

"I thought you liked it here—Jean said you've been at the club for years."

"I have—I did—but..." Benoît looked away, his gaze moving out the window, into the darkened street. "We're better than this place, Daniel. Better than a rundown club like Le Chat Rouge."

"You can't pin your hopes on me," Daniel said. "You hardly know me."

The look Benoît gave him, his dark eyes full of desire, heated his insides more than the whiskey.

"I'd like to know you better," Benoît said. He pushed back from the table and stood. "But we won't be able to do it here." His gaze promised Daniel more than just talk.

The little voice in his head told him that it'd never work. He'd fucked up all the other relationships he'd had. But if he stayed off the heroin, then just maybe…

He stood, and Benoît grinned. "Let's go to my place. Come on."

CHAPTER 4

Benoît's heart hammered in his chest as he preceded Daniel up the stairs to his tiny flat. Maybe the euphoria from their night's success was wearing off. Suddenly he didn't know why he'd propositioned Daniel so bluntly. But they were here now, and he didn't want to turn back. To hell with Fate. He hadn't felt this way in such a long time.

He unlocked the door, feeling Daniel's presence, his warmth, behind him. He reached back, laying a hand on Daniel's thigh, feeling the muscles shift under his touch. Daniel pressed forward, molding his body to Benoît's back. Benoît's breath caught in his throat.

"Second thoughts?" Daniel rasped in his ear. Benoît pushed open the door and they stumbled inside, clutching at each other. Daniel shoved him against the wall.

"Not now," he managed to say before their lips collided, an urgent groping in the dark. He fumbled for the light switch, but Daniel caught his hand, threading his fingers through Benoît's.

"Leave it off," Daniel said, his hips giving a sensual roll against Benoît. The wainscoting dug into Benoît's buttocks, but he didn't care as Daniel's erection pressed against his thigh. He fumbled with Daniel's belt, but Daniel pinned his hand against the wall.

Benoît struggled half-heartedly against the strong grip and Daniel chuckled. The sound went right to Benoît's groin. Daniel nipped at his neck, his tongue flicking out to trace the line of Benoît's jaw.

"Daniel," he managed to hiss before Daniel covered his lips in another deep kiss. He sagged against the wall. When they broke off, they were both breathing hard.

"Did you do this with all the other singers?" Daniel asked, easing his grip.

"Just you." Benoît turned his wrist and slid his hand free, clasping the back of Daniel's neck, feeling the silky short hair against his fingers. "Just you," he repeated. They kissed again and Benoît pushed off the wall, stumbling towards the bed. Desire burned in him and he tugged at Daniel's coat, pulling it down his arms and dropping it to the floor. By the time they reached the bed, Benoît was only wearing his trousers, and Daniel was down to his boxer shorts.

Benoît pushed Daniel down onto the bed, following closely. The bed creaked in protest at the added weight. He felt the muscles in Daniel's back flex and then he slid his hand under the elastic of Daniel's boxers, grasping at his ass. Daniel groaned in his ear, tearing at the waistband of Benoît's trousers, pulling them down his legs, and taking his briefs, too.

When Daniel's hand closed around his cock, Benoît thought he would come right then. Daniel swirled his thumb over the tip and Benoît saw stars behind his closed eyes. Two hard strokes, then a third, and Benoît arched his back, feeling the spasms up his vertebrae, exploding in brilliant colors. He felt the splatter of hot come on his belly and couldn't hold back a moan.

"Sorry, sorry," he gasped. Daniel muffled his apologies with a kiss.

"Don't be. We're not done yet."

Benoît tugged at his wet briefs, shucking them and mopping the mess from his stomach before dropping them over the side of the bed. His hands shook and he couldn't seem to catch his breath. Daniel slid down on the bed beside him and Benoît let his head fall onto Daniel's shoulder. He inhaled, finding the faint smell of cigarettes from the club, a hint of cologne, and an underlying, addicting fragrance that seemed to be Daniel's alone. A hunger rose in him.

"I didn't kill you, did I?" Daniel asked, his voice a murmur in Benoît's ear. He shifted on the bed and Benoît felt the slight breeze as Daniel's boxers joined his briefs on the floor. Benoît turned onto his side facing Daniel, tracing a path down Daniel's ribs, feeling over every bump, and when he reached the bottom of the rib cage, his hand slid down, and he felt the trail of hair. Lower, and he grasped Daniel's cock, provoking a moan. The moonlight filtered through the single window and by its light he could just see the edge of Daniel's nose, his parted lips, the slight shine of his forehead.

"Let me turn the light on," he said, taking his hand to the base of Daniel's cock, and up to the tip in a long stroke. He wanted to see Daniel fully, every inch of his lean body.

"Later," Daniel said hoarsely. "Don't you stop." His fingers scrabbled for purchase and he gripped Benoît's bicep hard enough to leave bruises. Benoît used his knee between Daniel's legs to push him onto his back, then he bent his head and placed a kiss on Daniel's sternum, tasting the smooth skin before he moved lower. He sat back on his haunches, kneeling between Daniel's legs. He paused.

"Do you want it?" A silly question, but he wanted to hear him, hear Daniel's need, know that Daniel wanted this as much as he did.

"Please," Daniel whispered, his voice seeming loud in the darkened room.

Benoît bent his head and his tongue flicked out, teasing the tip of Daniel's cock, tasting the pre-come there, the slight saltiness. Daniel lifted his hips, but Benoît moved back. He stroked the tops of Daniel's thighs, letting his fingers drag over the light hair, barely touching. Then again, except on his inner thighs. Daniel's whole body quivered like an animal on edge.

Benoît leaned forward again, and without warning, took Daniel's cock in his mouth, covering it completely, his nose tapping the trail of hair on Daniel's abdomen. Daniel gave a choked cry, almost a sob, his cock hardening further in Benoît's mouth. Benoît held it there a moment, letting Daniel come back down to earth before he slowly withdrew, the tip of his tongue dragging along the underside. When he reached the head, he paused, sucking harder, playing his tongue along the frenulum.

Daniel writhed on the sheets and Benoît held him down,

dipping his head again, feeling the tip of Daniel's cock press against the back of his throat. He repeated the motions several times, slowing to keep Daniel on the brink of orgasm, his breath rasping heavily, his cries a special music to Benoît's ears. He'd forgotten the sounds—the quiet grunt of effort when Daniel tried to lift his hips, the great intake of breath, the burst of exhalation, the panting. But the cries, the delicious desperation...he was hard again himself.

When Daniel's cries became a plaintive sound of need, Benoît took pity on him, taking him deep. Daniel thrust into his mouth and came. Benoît swallowed convulsively, sucking until Daniel's cock began to soften, until his cries became great gulping gasps for air.

He sat back, his jaw sore, his lips swollen, his cock hard and weeping. It wasn't enough. He wanted more from Daniel, wanted everything.

Daniel sprawled on the bed, boneless against the sheets, his fingers still twisted in the cotton.

"Come here," he said, his voice hoarse. He lifted one hand, catching Benoît's fingers and pulling him forward so they lay beside each other, damp skin pressed to damp skin.

Daniel shifted onto his side, running a hand down Benoît's chest, gently tweaking a nipple before going lower. Benoît hissed in a breath as Daniel stroked his cock, slow and purposeful. When Benoît shuddered, Daniel squeezed the base of his cock.

"Not yet," he said. "Not with what I want to do." He smiled then, a grin Benoît could just see in the shimmer of moonlight. Benoît grasped at the handle of the nightstand drawer. Daniel fished through the drawer's contents, pulling out a foil-wrapped condom and a bottle of lube. The condoms were new—Benoît had bought them hoping against hope that he'd be here, like this.

Daniel rose onto his knees, tearing open the packet. He sheathed Benoît's cock.

"I want you." Benoît took the lube from him as Daniel straddled his waist, pouring a bit into his hand before sliding his fingers between Daniel's legs, stroking him, teasing the ring of flesh. Daniel pressed against his fingers and Benoît inserted one, then a second.

Daniel's hand clasped his, pushing his fingers deeper. "You won't hurt me," he said.

"You sure?" It had been so long. Benoît felt out of practice.

"Perfectly." Daniel tugged at Benoît's hand and the pair of them stroked the rest of the lube over Benoît's condom-sheathed cock. Daniel inched forward, holding himself above Benoît.

Benoît watched as slowly, ever so slowly, Daniel lowered himself down. Benoît felt the snug pressure of Daniel's ass, and the heat. His hips jerked up and Daniel met his stroke. They rocked on the bed, Benoît coming up to a sitting position.

Daniel shifted, wrapping his legs around Benoît's waist. He tilted his hips back and forth and Benoît groaned with pleasure, his head falling onto Daniel's shoulder.

"You feel so good," Daniel whispered in his ear, dropping a kiss on his neck.

The tension and pleasure built until Benoît could hardly

stand it. He shook with need, his fingers sinking into Daniel's buttocks, forcing him closer, trying to get deeper. Daniel shuddered around him and Benoît could feel the perspiration slicking them both. Then he felt the hot pulse of Daniel's release between them. Daniel cried out and bit down on Benoît's shoulder as he came.

That sharp pain was what did it for Benoît. He came hard, balls deep in Daniel, gasping for breath.

Benoît wasn't sure how long they stayed like that, a tangle of limbs and sweat, but finally Daniel shifted and rose off him, staggering upright beside the bed. He stumbled into the bathroom and Benoît flopped back onto the bed after disposing of the condom. He couldn't move, and he didn't want to.

Daniel returned and Benoît shifted over to make room, but Daniel hesitated.

"Come on," Benoît said, lifting an arm. "Too late to get a cab now." He thought he saw Daniel smile, but in the dark he couldn't be sure. But he did slide into bed, curling up next to Benoît.

"Bonne nuit," Daniel said, punctuating his words with a yawn.

"Bonne nuit," Benoît echoed. It was a good night. It felt right, to have Daniel here beside him. He'd forgotten what it was like to fall asleep listening to another's breathing, next to his warmth. It was perfect.

The sound of the shower woke him. Daniel blinked sleepily, looking around the tiny studio apartment. He stretched out an arm, but the bed beside him was cold, though the mattress dipped, the slight indent from Benoît's body still there. It reassured him that he hadn't dreamt the whole thing—the drinks, the camaraderie, the sex. The lust. Maybe something more. Usually his lovers weren't as tender as Benoît, or so willing to see to more than their own pleasure.

Daniel eased from the bed, feeling the warm ache from last night's exertions. He stretched, reaching his arms up, his fingertips brushing the low ceiling. In the light from the single window he saw the darkened track marks on his arms, the faint discoloration of healing bruises, and the pockmarks from the unsuccessful attempts to hit a vein. He was hideous. Benoît would never want him in the light of day. He needed his clothes.

He turned abruptly, searching for his shirt, then saw he was too late. Benoît stood there, fresh from his shower, a towel wrapped round his waist, and his chest, with its light furring of dark hair, still damp with moisture. Daniel had seen that wide-eyed reaction before. He should have stayed away, kept to his own kind. Other addicts didn't care, or they considered the scars badges of honour in a twisted way. But straights, it disgusted them. He stooped to pick up his shirt, now irreparably wrinkled, and slipped it on, his hands shaking as he buttoned it.

"I'll just be on my way," he muttered, finding his trousers under Benoît's shirt.

"What did I do?" Benoît looked hurt, a flash of confusion passing over his kind features, the dark eyes that made Daniel's heart skip a beat when they looked at him with desire. There was no desire now.

Daniel didn't answer, just pulled on his trousers. When he looked up from buttoning the waistband, Benoît was right there beside him.

"Hold on." Benoît shifted to block Daniel's path to the door. He put out a hand, the heat from his palm a beacon of comfort against Daniel's cold body. The warmth seemed to sink through his shirt and into his chest. Daniel's resolve crumbled when he met Benoît's gaze. He tried to say something but the words were stuck in his throat. It would be easier to deal with rejection, easier to get angry.

But not this…tenderness. He didn't know what to do. Benoît's face blurred in his vision. No, he wouldn't break down in front of him. He couldn't. He never did that.

He turned away, but Benoît's touch didn't falter. The heat of his hand warmed the skin between Daniel's shoulder blades, and he had a fancy that the warmth spread through to join up with the warmth over his heart, creating a tiny, precious core.

Then Benoît stepped up behind him and it wasn't just a tiny core. It spread through his torso, down his hips and over his flesh like a waterfall. Benoît caught him about the waist as his knees weakened. They sank to the bed.

"Talk to me," Benoît said. "Sing to me, if it's easier." At that, Daniel managed a choked laugh.

"I don't know if I can."

"Tell me about these." Benoît's free hand traced over Daniel's sleeve, trailing warmth over the scars.

"Long story." Daniel cleared his throat, blinking away the tears.

"Which drugs, and how long? I'm a musician, after all, not an innocent."

Daniel thought hard, wondering where to start. "Hash, ecstasy, at least at first. Then a bit of cocaine when I needed something more. Then…" He hung his head. Benoît tightened his embrace. "Even the coke wasn't enough. My dealer gave me a sample, promised it would be the best ever."

"China white?" Benoît asked.

"Yeah. The cleanest stuff he had, the heroin he kept for his best clients. God, the high." Daniel shuddered. He didn't want to think about it. Thinking made him crave it, the euphoria, the release, letting go of the pain.

"Are you off it now?"

"Yes." The answer came out shakily, so he tried again. "Yes. That's why I came here." It was. Sort of.

Benoît regarded him seriously. "And you thought I'd hate you for it?"

"Everyone else has."

"Not me."

"You say that now," Daniel said.

"You've been the only one in years that has made me feel this way," Benoît said. Daniel gaped at him. No one had ever said that to him.

Ever.

"You deserve better."

"Let me decide that."

"I should just go—I couldn't stand it if you dropped me." Daniel shifted against Benoît's embrace, but Benoît held him tight.

"Take a chance. Tempt fate with me." Benoît kissed Daniel's neck, and this time his shudder was pleasure.

"What if I'm not what you want?" Daniel pressed. Benoît didn't understand, not really. "It's always there, Benoît. Sometimes it screams, demands, or like now, it only whispers. But I've never been free."

"What keeps you from listening to the screams?"

"I don't know. Sooner or later, I'll break. This time it just hasn't happened yet."

Benoît reclined on the bed, tugging Daniel down with him.

"I'll help you."

"Can you?" Daniel wanted to believe him.

"Trust me." Benoît cupped his cheek and Daniel closed his eyes at the caress. "I'll keep your mind on other things." His low chuckle made Daniel's heart race.

"Like what?" he asked, breathless.

Benoît kissed him.

CHAPTER 5

As he dressed for work, moving about carefully in his tiny room above Le Chat Rouge, Daniel couldn't help the smile that kept sneaking onto his face. He'd only just left Benoît, and he'd see him again soon. If only they didn't have to get through an evening's performance first.

They'd fallen into a sort of rhythm, a comforting habit. After the encore, they'd go to the café for a brandy, then back to Benoît's. Sometimes they'd linger at the café till closing, and others, they'd rush back, barely able to keep their clothes on long enough to get into the studio flat.

Daniel left his bow tie hanging. Benoît always did a better job of tying it. Or he'd leave it loose, like some playboy—

A stern knock sounded on the door.

Daniel took a single step over and pulled it open. Jean stood there, pristine as always in his starched shirt and waistcoat. His tie was perfectly straight, of course.

"Royale wants to see you." He turned on his heel. When

Daniel didn't move, he let another word go over his shoulder. "Now."

The closer he got to Royale's office, the thicker the smoke, and the stronger the smell. Jean didn't seem to be affected, but Daniel wrinkled his nose and then tried to breathe shallowly. Royale must have been stewing in there all day—usually the smoke only got like this near to closing.

Jean opened the door and ushered Daniel inside. Rather than leave, he stepped in behind Daniel, forcing him forward, closer to Royale.

Royale had settled his bulk behind his desk and he fiddled with a laptop, watching the screen intently. A cigar burned in the ashtray and a dirty plate sat next to it, along with a half-full snifter of cognac and an empty glass of wine.

Jean nudged Daniel towards the chair in front of Royale's desk, and he sat, though he didn't relax. He heard the door shut, and when he glanced back, he saw Jean leaning against it.

"Thank you for coming," Royale said, his deep voice raspy. He coughed into a handkerchief, then stuffed it into a pocket of his dark suit. His eyes still on the screen, he patted his thinning, reddish hair.

Daniel waited, and finally Royale deigned to look at him.

"You've done well here," he said, and when Daniel began to speak, held up a hand. "Better than I'd expected, given your history."

"I argued against hiring you," Jean remarked. Royale shot

him a look, but Daniel didn't turn to see its effect on the maître'd.

"Do I get a raise?" Daniel asked, trying to keep from sounding impertinent. He doubted he was here for that reason. Royale didn't seem like the sort to go around giving bonuses.

"As part of your continued employment here," Royale said, as if he hadn't heard Daniel's question, "I require repayment of the faith I've shown in you." He picked up his cigar.

Daniel's stomach did a nervous flop.

"My associate in Marseille has a parcel for me, and our regular courier is unavailable," Royale said. "I'll need you to go pick it up."

"But, I can't go back—"

"Your dealer friend's in prison," Jean interrupted. "Don't be a coward."

"Once you pick up the parcel, you'll bring it back here. You'll leave tomorrow morning—we can spare you for Sunday night. And I expect you in my office by Tuesday morning." Royale idly blew a smoke ring towards the ceiling.

"But I can't go back," Daniel protested. The dealer wasn't his only worry. Being home made him vulnerable.

"It's your choice," Royale said, surprisingly genial. "But Valois, you remember your old boss, mentioned he has some information the cops might want. Something about a young man dying?" Royale turned his attention to his laptop again. "Now, what was his name? I can never remember, but he was a pretty little thing, wasn't he?"

Daniel remembered. The bile rose in his throat and he swallowed it back. He hadn't known the heroin he'd given Marcel had been spiked. It looked the same as always, and he'd thought nothing of it.

"Valois says he's been questioned," Royale said, "about that poor boy's death. The cops want to find out who gave him those drugs, and who left him to die. I'd guess prison would be in your near future." He shrugged. "Pity to waste such talent."

He couldn't say no. If he could, he'd tell Royale off, storm out of the office, out of the club. "When do I leave?" Daniel forced himself to say the words. He had no other choice.

"Jean will fill you in," Royale said, waving a hand. If he could do it without ending up in the Seine, Daniel would have laid Royale out with his fist. He was just another cog in the machine. "Now go on, it's almost showtime. We wouldn't want to disappoint your adoring fans."

Daniel rose and Jean opened the door, following him out.

"I'll talk to you afterwards," Jean said. "Don't go anywhere."

When Daniel reached the stage, the band was there. Benoît gave him a wink, but Daniel didn't wink back like he usually did. There was a sour taste in his mouth and his stomach churned. He had to go back. Back there. He managed a slight smile and shake of his head when Benoît looked worried, but Daniel was sure his reassurances were unconvincing.

At the break, Daniel retreated to the dressing room instead of heading to the bar for a drink. Usually he didn't mind the women fawning over him, but he couldn't concentrate. He shut the door and slumped in the chair. Maybe he could get in and out of Marseille without getting in trouble. Or, at the very least, he could go see Laure and avoid the rest. He'd have to stay away from his usual haunts, do what he came to do, and get the hell out and back to Paris.

The door swung open behind him, letting in a rush of noise and conversation. Daniel glanced up into the mirror. Benoît stood there, as he'd expected. His dark eyes radiated concern and Daniel almost wished Benoît wasn't there, that he didn't exist. It'd be easier without ties, easier without emotion.

Benoît touched his shoulder in passing and squeezed in front of Daniel, leaning against the vanity table.

"Bad day?" Benoît asked.

How to explain? Did Benoît have any idea about his employer? Royale wasn't small time. Daniel ducked his head, rubbing the back of his neck.

"I have to go back home."

He heard Benoît's quick intake of breath. "When?"

"Tomorrow."

"When were you going to tell me?"

Daniel looked up. He'd never seen Benoît look so stricken.

"I only just found out today. I won't be gone forever," Daniel said. "Just a few days." Benoît's expression calmed. "Family stuff. It can't wait."

The lie burned on his tongue, and Daniel hated to do it, but Royale had been clear, even if he hadn't said it outright. No one could know.

"You had me worried," Benoît said, his tone gently scolding. He leaned forward, cupping Daniel's cheek. Daniel closed his eyes, letting the warmth of Benoît's touch sink into his skin, knowing he gravitated towards the other man like a moth to a flame. But this flame didn't hurt. Benoît was the wood stove in a country house, the heart of him. Daniel didn't know how he'd manage without Benoît now.

Daniel opened his eyes. Benoît glanced at his watch. "I wish we had longer."

"Why?" The question slipped out. Benoît grinned.

"Because." He bent forward and caught Daniel's mouth in a hard, passionate kiss. Daniel groaned, clutching at Benoît's arms, tugging him closer. To hell with the next set.

A fist pounded on the door and they broke apart. Benoît raked a hand through his hair as he turned to face the mirror.

"We don't look like we've been snogging," he said.

"A pity," Daniel replied. He wanted to see Benoît's lips swollen from his kisses, know that he'd been the one to do it.

"Later," Benoît said. "Only one more set."

Benoît sat at the piano still, though the customers had all left, and even Serge and Patrice had gone. He waited for Daniel to square his absence with Jean and Royale, and it was taking longer than he'd expected. Likely Jean was arguing against Daniel returning to Marseille. Though he'd only be gone a couple of days, Benoît couldn't help but worry, just a little. After all, Marseille was Daniel's home—family, ex-lovers… He refocused on the music. He wouldn't think of that. He trusted Daniel.

He segued from a Jacques Brel tune into something all his own. He'd been working on it for a while, but hadn't gotten much further than the first verse. He needed a hook, something that would stay with an audience long after they'd gone home. He shifted into a minor key, playing a series of chords. Liking the combination, he tried it again, adding in a melody with his right hand. A note jarred and he started over, until the music flowed, the melody and chords beginning to work in harmony.

He heard voices and he jotted down the chord changes and the basic melody onto a scrap of blank sheet music. Daniel emerged from the back hall, followed by Jean. He made a motion with his hand and Benoît tucked the paper into his music book and closed the fallboard. That could wait. Right now, he wanted Daniel. Two days away from him was too long.

Benoît caught up to Daniel at the front door, slipping his hand into Daniel's, squeezing his fingers. He glanced back. Jean raised a brow, but said nothing. Then they were out on the street in the cool night air, and Jean was forgotten.

"Drink?" Benoît asked, though in truth he wanted Daniel more than he wanted a drink. Daniel seemed to read his thoughts— or maybe he'd been thinking the same thing.

"Home."

They managed to stave off their desire until Benoît opened the door, but then the need overflowed. Benoît's hands shook as he undid his bow tie and unbuttoned his shirt, pulling it from the waistband of his trousers. When he glanced up, Daniel was doing the same.

"Bet I'll beat you," he said, even as he fumbled with his cufflinks.

Daniel chuckled. "Bet you won't."

He didn't defeat Daniel, but it was a game with two winners. They tumbled onto the bed, skin against skin, arms and legs entwined. He wouldn't be able to do this tomorrow night, or the next. Strange how a few weeks had changed everything.

"Will you miss me while you're away?" Benoît asked, his voice surprisingly hoarse. It had meant to be a flippant, teasing question. Daniel rested his forehead against Benoît's and their gazes locked, blue and brown. There was sadness there, in Daniel's eyes, but love, too.

"Every moment."

CHAPTER 6

In the morning, it took all Daniel had to leave Benoît behind. He shouldered his duffel, much lighter now since he'd left most of his stuff at Benoît's, and caught the metro at Abbesses, switching at Saint-Lazare amongst all the business-people, and continuing on to Gare de Lyon.

He checked the inside pocket of his leather jacket again, fingering the ticket there.

"Royale's contact, Raoul, won't make it to Marseille until midday on Monday," Jean had said, "but Royale didn't want to change your ticket. Consider it a bit of a holiday."

A holiday. He shook his head. He couldn't afford a holiday, but perhaps his old schoolfriend Laure would still be working at the café and tabac shop in La Savine. If she'd see him, that is. She and Marcel had been close.

Daniel found the TGV express to Marseille and validated his ticket. He headed down the platform and went aboard the train. He found his seat in the second-class carriage—a window seat, thankfully, though Royale hadn't been the least bit generous—and settled in, stowing his duffel under the seat in front of him. Benoît had lent him a book, a crime thriller by Jo Nesbø, but the trip south took over three hours. He wouldn't start it now.

He glanced out the window, looking down at the crowd milling about, the mix of posh and destitute. A woman with the poise of a fashion model caught his eye. She was perfectly done up, from the band of her cap to the shiny tips of her stilettos. One hand rested on the handle of her luggage, and she nattered into her mobile phone. Her purse, a trendy monstrosity, was partly open and he watched as a young man took notice, drifting closer to her in the crowd. He looked like most other young men of his age—jeans, trainers, slightly worn, a day's growth of patchy stubble on his boyish face. His olive-skinned hand slithered into her bag, then out, quick as could be. If Daniel hadn't known what to look for, he would have missed it.

The boy melted back into the crowd, probably heading to the exit. The woman wouldn't notice her pocketbook missing until she got on the train. He knew he should be more sympathetic, but he remembered his own youth, always desperate for cash. The kid looked in better shape than he'd been at that age. He'd been looking for his next fix.

Daniel rubbed his hands down his thighs. He didn't need a fix now, he told himself. He'd be fine. But the thought was in his head and he felt a prickle of sweat under his arms. Think of something else. Under his breath, he began to sing a Hoagy Carmichael tune Benoît liked to play, 'Am I Blue?', tapping his fingers to the non-existent percussion, imagining Benoît at his piano. He could hear the music clearly in his mind, see the little flourishes Benoît made at the chorus.

Benoît.

He knew he was lovesick. Already he missed Benoît. He shouldn't. They hadn't known each other long, a month, perhaps. But somehow, Benoît had found his way in, and now Daniel felt incomplete. Vulnerable.

While he'd been musing, the train had filled. An older, rotund woman lumbered down the aisle and headed straight for the extra seat next to Daniel. She sat with a heavy thump and a sigh, her thighs spilling over the edge of her seat and onto his. Her perfume was heavy, a sort of Chanel knock-off, and Daniel shrank away from her.

The train pulled out of the station and he turned to look out the window, seeing the stone walls crawl by, the graffiti colourful and varied. The woman next to him shifted in her seat. Once the train began to pick up speed, Daniel rose to his feet, grabbing his duffel. He'd find a free spot in the bar car.

"Pardon, madame."

The woman harrumphed, but rose to let him out. He made his way down the aisle and through the connecting door. Most travelers had yet to leave their seats and the bar car was practically empty. There was nowhere to sit, but he bought a bottle of Vittel and leaned on the small side counter where he could watch the scenery pass by. He stashed his duffel at his feet. He'd linger as long as he could before he'd go back to endure his seat partner.

"Merde!"

He glanced over. The young woman, the model he'd seen on the platform earlier, was digging through her purse in frustration. The bar attendant tapped his fingers on the counter.

"But I just had it," the woman said. She turned away from the bar dispiritedly, her delicate shoulders slumping.

"It could have been pickpockets," Daniel said. The woman glanced at him.

"It must have been. I can call and cancel all my cards, but I don't have any cash."

"Can I buy you something?" He felt guilty for having seen the theft, but there was nothing he could have done to stop it.

She gave him an unexpectedly tremulous smile, and underneath all the glamour was an ordinary woman, not an unapproachable model. Prior to Benoît, he might have hit on her, but though he found her attractive, there was no spark.

"Merci," she said. "I'll just have a bottle of water."

Daniel dug in his pocket and paid the barman. The woman cracked open the bottle and took a long drink.

"Better?" he asked.

"It helps. Thank you. That was very kind."

"De rien. You should try calling the rail company; maybe a worker at Gare de Lyon found your pocketbook."

She pulled out her phone with a sigh. "It's probably long gone by now, but it's worth a try." She gave him another smile, but already she was distracted.

"Bonne chance," he said, raising his bottle of water. She smiled again and moved away, talking rapidly into her mobile. He turned his gaze back to the window but his mind was elsewhere.

The graffiti of the city finally gave way to the countryside and he stared out over the fields and trees, not really seeing them. His stomach fluttered and his grip on the water bottle tightened. He had too much time to kill in Marseille. If he could step off the train right this moment, he would, even if it meant walking back to Paris. Though he might be able to stay clear of trouble, just being back would be hard enough.

The train trundled into the station and Daniel gathered up his duffel. He'd retreated to his seat for the last hour, to the disapproval of the woman next to him. She'd spread her hand luggage out into both seats and was quite perturbed to have to give up her extra space. She took her time gathering her things and he tried not to fidget as he waited to get past her.

Once out on the platform, he followed the crowd into the terminal, slipping through the gaps, impatient to be out of the building. He pushed open the door and stepped outside. The afternoon sun beat down on the stone plaza and the heat warmed him to his bones. He took a deep breath. He could smell the sea, the blue Mediterranean not far away. He took his time walking down the steps, remembering when he'd left, not saying goodbye to anyone before he caught the TGV to Paris and his new job. He should go back to La Savine, pop into the old café. Laure would still be there, waiting tables. If she didn't hate him. Marcel had nearly been her fiancé, and if not for Daniel, she'd still have him.

Daniel turned westward. He could catch the metro to

Bougainville and then the bus out to La Savine, but not yet. The need twinged in him, but he ignored it. A walk would do him good.

He crossed the road and followed it along, heading in the general direction of the port. He needed to see the water again, feel the sea breeze. He skirted Place Thiars, knowing it would be thronged with tourists. The Quai Rive Neuve was busy, but he strolled along, watching the boats bobbing at their moorings, their masts like a forest of bare trees. The sun glinted off the water, making him squint. When he reached the end of the marina, he continued along the rue des Catalans, pausing at the edge of the crowded beach.

He missed this in Paris. The Seine didn't have the same impact as this expanse of blue. He leaned on the rail. Benoît should see this. Had he ever? Daniel wanted Benoît here beside him. He wanted to make new memories here to clear away the old. He, Laure, and Marcel had come down to the water's edge many a time, spending hours in the sun, on the sand, among all the people. He knew this area of Marseille as intimately as La Savine. He grimaced and turned away. Impossible to go back. It hurt too much to remember. Things were so different then.

Daniel retraced his steps. To have Benoît here with him, he'd go to the most touristy restaurant in Place Thiars, or the most obscure little club, whatever Benoît wanted. But he wasn't here. Daniel picked up his pace. No point in putting things off any further. He headed to the nearest metro stop for line 2, at Noailles. He was sweating by the time he reached the boulevard Garibaldi, and he wiped a hand across his forehead. His jacket was over one arm, but it was hot just carrying the leather.

Bougainville was the end of the line, and Daniel didn't even have to think as his feet took him to the bus stop. Number 30, La Savine. The others waiting for the bus were a mixed lot. He heard several languages being spoken, including a pair of women who spoke softly in Arabic, and some young men who spoke an African dialect he wasn't familiar with. An older man talked rapidly in Italian, his mobile held tight to one ear as he paced back and forth.

Daniel shoved his hands in his pockets. His fingers closed around some crumpled plastic and the smooth, small shape of the remaining joint he'd bought off the boys at Les Halles. A craving shot through him, intense and needy, and he closed his eyes against the onslaught.

Think of Benoît.

He pictured Benoît at his piano, playing that medley of Casablanca songs he'd done up, his curly dark hair shining under the stage lights, his fingers moving over the keys, his head bobbing in time to the music, a habit he had. Daniel's need shifted, changed. He wanted Benoît under him on the bed, his mouth opening on a moan, his legs splayed wide.

Daniel opened his eyes. If only.

The bus pulled up and he waited in line, shuffling forward with the others. He sat near the back, keeping his duffel on his lap. There were all sorts here and he didn't want to lose anything to a quick-fingered fellow passenger. He settled back for the ride. It would be a long one.

The bus shuddered to a stop at the crossroads of the boulevard de la Savine, and the Chemin du Vallon des Tuves. His old turf. Already it felt strange to him, though he hadn't been gone very long. Had Paris really affected him that much?

Daniel rose and disembarked after a couple of tall African men, who talked to each other in heavily accented, rapid-fire French. The bus pulled away after he stepped off, and the setting sun was hot as ever in this unsheltered spot. He re-folded his jacket over his arm, and swung his duffel over his shoulder. Then he started walking, past garages and gated properties and the odd vacant lot. The houses were worn and tired, their paint faded, weeds growing from between the cracks in the sidewalk.

It didn't take long to get to the café, the tabac sign a bright red and white. A few men sat at the tables outside, smoking and talking. He glanced through the doorway. A slender young woman, her mousy hair pulled back into a messy bun, wiped tables with a rag. She paused and straightened, pushing hair off her forehead. Laure.

Daniel went in. Laure turned and her tight-lipped expression faded. A smile broke over her features and then she was the prettiest girl he'd ever seen. She hurried over and gave him a hug so hard he thought he'd almost cracked a rib.

"Oof," he said, playfully, and Laure let go, smacking him on the shoulder.

"When did you get back? You never told anyone you were coming," she said, half-scolding.

"It was unexpected." He rubbed his shoulder where she'd hit him. "If I'd known you were going to abuse me, I'd have stayed in Paris."

She stuck her tongue out at him and he laughed. She hadn't changed. It was as if nothing had ever happened, as if Marcel would walk in that door and it would be as it was.

Marcel. He should be here, hanging around, chatting with the old men outside as he waited for Laure to get off her shift, cracking jokes.

Laure looked at him, and her smile faded, as if she knew what he was thinking.

"Ça va?" Daniel asked, keeping his voice soft.

Laure shrugged. "Pas mal." She took his hand and he followed her to the back of the café, to a table near the kitchen. "I'm off early today, just wait here."

He pulled out a chair and sat. She finished cleaning the remaining tables, then the bar, then she swept the floor. On her way into the back, she untied the apron she wore over her snug dark jeans and sleeveless shirt. He heard her call out to the chef, the owner, but couldn't hear the man's reply.

Five minutes later, Laure returned, holding a small leather purse and a light jacket.

"Maman went back to Algiers to stay with Tante," Laure said, "so we'll have the place to ourselves."

They walked up the hill along boulevard du Bosphore, the viaduct looming to their left. Even though parts of La Savine were rundown, Daniel had always loved the viaduct. As a kid he'd oriented himself by its landmark, and he did it now. Another couple hundred metres and they'd reach the highrise apartment Laure shared with her mother. Some of the apartments were still in good shape, but most had seen better years, rented by absentee landlords and occupied by a string of tenants.

Laure pushed open the door. "It's messy," she said. "I've been working long hours since Maman left, and haven't had time."

It was bigger than his tiny room at Le Chat Rouge and bigger than Benoît's studio flat. He didn't mind. Laure went to the window and cracked it open.

"Air conditioner died," she said by way of explanation. She kicked off her shoes as she came back towards the door. "Make yourself at home. I need to clean up."

She retreated to the bedroom and Daniel let his duffel and jacket fall to the floor. He stepped over to the window and peered out. Same old place, same old view. It was comforting in a way, but not quite right. He turned away and dropped to the sagging sofa. It creaked under his weight and the springs had too much give. Any more and his ass would be on the linoleum. He leaned back.

The place was plain, simple, the room a pale off-white, a cluster of family photos in frames tacked up on one wall, and an old landscape painting hung over the small television. A round wooden table and chairs peeked out from the snug kitchen nook. Dishes were piled there, empty glasses and plates with sticky knives and forks. She really hadn't been cleaning.

Daniel heard the shower running. He leveraged himself off the sofa. Maybe if he was a good guest, she'd take pity on him and let him stay the night. He didn't want to go back into the city to a hotel. He couldn't afford it, and he didn't want to be alone.

He was nearly finished with the dishes when Laure returned, her long hair hanging in a damp line down her back, clad in a black skirt and tank top.

"Daniel," she said reprovingly as she came into the kitchen, "you shouldn't have."

He shrugged and dried the last dish before putting it in the cupboard. "Had to do something to keep busy." The work had kept his mind off of Benoît, and off of the drugs. The last time he'd been in this apartment, he'd been in withdrawal, sweating and in pain. Laure's mother had been there, giving him a wide berth—as much as she could in the small apartment.

"How have you been?" Laure leaned on the door frame, her arms crossed in front of her. Her gaze was searching, concerned. "You look well. I wish you'd called."

Daniel hung the dish towel off the knob of a cupboard door. "I found a job in Paris, singing in a club. It's steady."

"Do you like it?"

"Yeah." He smiled, thinking of Benoît.

"Good. Don't blame yourself for Marcel, Daniel. You know as well as I do that he'd have gotten the drugs off someone else if it hadn't been you."

Daniel winced. Trust Laure to be direct. But no matter what she said, Marcel would be alive today if it wasn't for him.

"But it did happen," he said, turning away. The sun shone through the dusty kitchen window, creating a warm patch on the counter. His hand rested there but he didn't feel the heat. His fingers were like ice.

Laure sighed. He heard her footsteps on the linoleum, then her arms came around him, gently squeezing him around the middle. Her head rested on his back, between his shoulder blades. She'd always been there for him, even though Marcel had been her boyfriend, almost her fiancé. Her Maman had been planning their marriage for years.

"If it's anyone's fault, it's mine," Laure said, her voice muffled against his back. "I should have tried harder to get him off the heroin."

Daniel turned in her embrace, putting his arms around her.

"We're quite a pair," he said. He cupped the back of her head and they stood there for several minutes before breaking apart.

Laure scrubbed at her eyes. "Now that you're here, we should go out. There's a party down on the Chemin de Tuileries. The DJs go out all night."

"Maybe."

"It's better than hanging around here." She gestured at the empty walls, the worn furniture.

"All right." Daniel yawned.

"You can take the bed," Laure told him. "We'll crash for a bit, then head out later."

"I can take the couch," Daniel replied.

"Fine, we'll both take the bed," Laure decided. "You'd just better not snore."

"Je te promets." He followed Laure into the bedroom. The queen-size bed would fit them both. He shucked his jeans and shirt and lay down in his boxers, stretching out. Laure curled up on the other side of the bed.

"I'm glad you're back," she said, her voice barely a whisper. "I missed you."

CHAPTER 7

Benoît sat back from the piano. He was glad for the break; the night seemed to drag, the music felt dull and lifeless, and he didn't want to think of going home to an empty bed. When he descended the stairs at the side of the stage, a man met him at the bottom, looking eager. He wore a well-tailored suit, with gold cufflinks that glinted at his wrists, and a heavy gold wristwatch. He was balding slightly at the temples, but his greying hair made him look distinguished. He held out his hand and Benoît took it. The man had a strong handshake, confident.

"I'm Eric James, a talent agent from New York. Have you considered playing at the Birdland? You might not know it, but it's—"

"Oui, je sais Le Birdland," Benoît said, giving the man a smile to make up for the interruption. "It's legendary."

"Well yes, it is." For a moment, James looked abashed, but he recovered with aplomb.

"Drink?" Benoît offered. At the bar, James ordered a beer from Edouard. Benoît had his usual brandy. They retreated to Eric's table.

"We don't offer this to very many musicians, as much as we'd like to," James said. "But you, and the singer—"

"Daniel Marceau," Benoît supplied.

"Do you think you'd be able to do a week or two's booking? Say, in a couple of months time, or as soon as we can arrange the visas? We just had another group cancel—their singer needed surgery, or something." James shrugged and pulled a card from his pocket.

"I would love to," Benoît said. His heart raced and he had to keep himself from tightening his grasp on the delicate brandy snifter.

"And Mr. Marceau?" James asked. He took a deep draught of his beer.

"He's back Tuesday," Benoît replied.

"Let me know when you can," James said. "The sooner the better, so we can get everything arranged."

"Bien sûr." Daniel would be thrilled, Benoît knew it. America, and the Birdland—one of jazz's top venues. Benoît tucked James's card into the inside pocket of his jacket.

"You deserve a chance," James said. "You could be famous, and playing in better places than this." He indicated the dark burgundy walls with their dusty brass sconces, the aged furniture and the tatty and worn velvet covering the banquettes.

"It pays the bills." Benoît didn't want to explain his own lack of motivation, the lethargy that had kept him here. He didn't feel it now. He imagined walking in Times Square with Daniel, or in Central Park on a sunny afternoon, hand in hand.

He gulped down his brandy. Time to go back to work, if he could manage to concentrate.

"Keep in touch," James said as Benoît rose.

"You can count on it." Benoît headed back to the stage, feeling as if he were walking on air.

Benoît's hand was on him, tightening around his cock, bringing him to the brink. Daniel moaned. His eyes snapped open.

He was in an unfamiliar, yet familiar, bed, staring at a ceiling with a crack running down the centre, and there was a hand in his boxer shorts, but it wasn't Benoît's. He turned his head.

Laure lay next to him, her mousy hair spread over the pillow, her eyes half-closed.

"Laure, stop." Daniel gently took her wrist, pulling her hand away.

"But—" Laure's voice quavered. "You loved being woken that way." She shifted closer, the heat of her pressing along his right side. It would be so easy. Before Marcel, since the lycée, they'd been more than friends, not quite dating, but not just friends. He knew her body as well as his own, almost.

"I've met someone," he said, sitting up and scrubbing a hand over his face. "It wouldn't be right." He swung his legs over the side of the bed, his feet hitting the cold linoleum.

The mattress creaked and shifted as Laure moved away from him, rising from the other side of the bed, pushing her hair away from her face as she stalked from the room. Daniel rose and stretched. His erection tented the front of his boxers and he didn't want to go out into the living room to talk to Laure when he sported so obvious an indication of his arousal.

He paced to the window, raising the dusty venetian blind. He cracked open the sash and took a deep breath. He should have told her right away, and he should have slept on the sofa.

Daniel turned away from the window, scooping his jeans from the floor and pulling them on, then grabbing his shirt. In bare feet, he walked into the other room.

Laure was in the kitchen, her back to him, putting a moka pot on the stove to make espresso.

"I'm sorry, Laure," he said. She didn't acknowledge him, but he saw her grip the edge of the counter. "I should have said something."

Her shoulders drooped and she seemed to sink into herself. He thought he heard her shaky intake of breath, and her body went rigid. When he came up beside her, he saw the tears streaking her cheeks, her lips pressed together as if she could hold in the pain. He put an arm over her stiff shoulders. At first she resisted, but then she leaned into him. He embraced her and she sobbed into his shirt, drenching the cotton. He stroked her back and held her until her tears subsided.

"I'm happy for you," she said in a voice made thick with her sorrow, muffled by his shirt, "but Daniel, I'm so alone. You don't understand. Marcel, Maman, and you—you all left me." Her confession triggered more sobs and Daniel's chest tightened, his heart in his throat. He closed his eyes against the burn of his own tears and held her until she'd finally cried herself out.

Laure shifted in his arms and he looked down. Her face was tear-stained and blotchy.

"Why don't you come to Paris?" he asked gently, carefully. She shook her head.

"I couldn't. I promised Maman I'd look after the place for her. And you don't want me there anyway—I'd interfere with your love affair." She said this last bit with forced gaiety.

"I mean it," he said.

"I know." She stepped away from him, wiping her eyes. "I hope you won't leave because of this."

"I have things to do tomorrow, and a TGV ticket back to Paris later, but until then, I'm here."

"Good." Laure smiled, but it was shaky, her chin wobbling a moment. "Then you will come out with me tonight? We'll dance the night away like we used to."

Daniel didn't really want to go, but if it would make Laure happy, it was the least he could do.

"All right." He tugged at his shirt. "I need a shower first. And fresh clothes."

"I ruined your shirt," Laure said.

"I have a spare." He headed towards the bathroom.

"When you're done, we can eat," Laure said, her voice carrying down the hallway. He heard the clang of pots as he grabbed his duffel and shut the bathroom door. Just like old times.

CHAPTER 8

Before he left Le Chat Rouge for the night, Benoît surreptitiously checked his pocket for Eric James's card. Royale wouldn't like it, but to hell with him. After the Birdland, he and Daniel could go anywhere. He had a bit of money saved. They could find work somewhere else, maybe even leave Paris for good. The world was theirs. Him and Daniel. Daniel and him.

The thought carried him home, and he wanted to call Daniel, tell him the news. He looked at his watch. Too late. He'd tell him tomorrow. Or maybe meet him at Gare de Lyon and tell him in person. That's what he would do. He knew Daniel's arrival time, though it seemed so far away, now.

Benoît hung up his suit, making sure to take James's card from his pocket, placing it on the beside table. It lay there under the lamp like a sort of talisman, a ticket to better things. Once they'd played the Birdland they could try other clubs in New York, or move onto Washington, D.C., or forsake the rest of America altogether and go north to Montreal. And then? London? Sera and Marc were making a go of it there. They might have some contacts.

Benoît pulled his shirt over his head and let it drop. If only he could talk to Daniel right now. He itched to see him. He glanced over. The bed sat empty, the covers half off the way he'd left it earlier. Daniel's side would stay empty tonight.

Daniel's side.

He was amazed at himself. It hadn't been too long ago when his bed was always empty.

Was this what love felt like?

He headed to the bathroom for a shower, humming to himself.

Daniel kept pace with Laure as they headed down to the Chemin des Tuileries. As they got closer, he could hear the thudding bass. Laure practically skipped beside him. She seemed to have regained her good mood. She'd done up her hair into a thick braid and made herself up. Though she wore flats, she was clad in a tight-fitting, sexy dress. She was ready to dance, she'd said.

Daniel hadn't bothered to dress up. He'd changed into another white t-shirt and wore the same jeans as earlier. He wasn't here to pull anyone. He'd stay as long as Laure wanted, and that was all. She'd been right—he'd left without even considering how much it would hurt her. He'd make it up to her if he could, and if going to a rave, with its deafening music and crowds was what he had to do, then he would.

They joined a growing crowd of young people trickling

into the venue, its entrance tightly controlled by a pair of thickly-muscled security men. A bit much for a rave, he thought, but then Laure had paid their cover and they were through, into a loud, cavernous room. Lights pulsed over the walls, and he couldn't hear a thing over the music, a pounding dance beat. Laure tugged on his hand, dragging him into the centre of the crowd, already gyrating to the music. He felt stiff in comparison, but slowly he relaxed.

Laure grinned at him as they danced, then closed her eyes and threw her head back. She seemed to lose all concept of where she was, but he couldn't do the same. When she began to shift away from him, he tapped her shoulder. She opened her eyes.

"Outside," he mouthed, and she nodded. Daniel pushed his way through the dancers, the music pounding in his ears. He broke free of the clutch of writhing bodies and pushed open a door.

He found himself on the far side of the warehouse, the breeze cooling the evening air. He took a deep breath, but instead of freshness, he smelled hashish. With his hand on the door, he considered going back inside, but the music hadn't abated. Better to stay out here instead. A bit of hashish smoke wouldn't bother him. He wouldn't let it.

A couple of guys in jeans and trainers stood a few feet away, the smoke curling from the joints they held. Daniel couldn't see them well in the dim glow from the security light across the way, but he saw the one man gesture to him.

"Voulez-vous fumer avec nous?"

Daniel hesitated, then walked over. The man offered him the joint, but he shook his head. The man offered again, looking confused at Daniel's denial.

One toke wouldn't hurt, Daniel thought. He took the joint. The man grinned.

"C'est le meilleur," he boasted. Daniel inhaled. He felt a slight buzz. No, not the best he'd ever had. He gave the joint back.

"Merci." He remembered the joint from the other week, still in the plastic bag in his pocket. He pulled it out, straightening the crooked paper. With the buzz from it, he could stand going back into the warehouse for the rest of the night. He lit up.

After they finished Daniel's joint, his new friends, Pierre and Mathieu, complimented him on his taste in drugs.

"Where did you get such good hashish?" Mathieu wanted to know.

"Paris."

"Have any more?" Pierre asked. Daniel shook his head. Pierre frowned.

Mathieu dug in his pocket, coming up with a folded tab of aluminum foil. He unfolded it with the precision of a surgeon, revealing a small amount of white powder. He glanced up at Daniel.

"Want some?"

Daniel swallowed.

Pierre took a €5 note from his wallet and rolled it into a tube. Mathieu hunkered down against the side of the warehouse, blocking the wind so that none of the drug would be wasted. Pierre bent in, snorting up some of the powder. Then he held out the rolled up note to Daniel.

"Be a shame to miss this," he said. "Best China white ever." He sniffed and rubbed his nose, taking a deep breath before he slid to the ground, propping himself against the wall. The €5 note hung limply in his hand.

"Come on," Mathieu said, bending to take the note from Pierre's hand. "The party gets better with this."

Daniel stepped forward. The money felt slick against his fingers and he could feel the ridge of the print. It seemed so familiar.

The craving hit him like a truck, his hands trembling so badly he nearly dropped the roll. Every nerve in his body screamed out for that sweet bliss, the euphoria to take away all the pain. The world seemed to narrow until all he could see was the glint of the foil in Mathieu's hand.

He bent closer. Just one little sniff. It would quiet the cravings, he knew it would. He put the tube to his nose and inhaled.

It didn't hit him right away. But then he felt the calm, the looseness in his limbs, and he lowered himself clumsily to the ground before he fell. The calm turned to warmth, the warmth to the euphoria his body craved and demanded. It hadn't forgotten the feeling, this bliss, even though he'd denied it for several months.

And he'd thought he could manage without it. He pushed up on his elbow, seeing Mathieu beside him, holding the crumpled foil. He reached out, plucked it from Mathieu's limp fingers, and peered at it. A bit of powder still clung to the inside, so Daniel dampened a fingertip to lift it up, sucking the powder into his mouth. It was bitter, but he felt the zing, the frisson as it joined the heroin already in his system.

He laid back on the grass. Pure bliss.

An insistent beeping woke Daniel, knifing into his brain. With his eyes closed, he groped for his phone, his fingers sliding over the dull plastic. He cracked open one eye to look at the time.

Nine o'clock.

He groaned and sat up, his head spinning. He was on a sofa, a blanket crumpled at the end, his jeans still on but his shirt and shoes in a pile on the linoleum. For a moment he didn't remember where he was, but Laure came out of the bedroom, her hair in tangles and smudges around her eyes from her mascara, and he remembered. She wore a pink frilly robe, the lace hem dangling at one corner where it had pulled away from the fabric. She didn't say a word to him, merely gave him a glance as she made her way to the kitchen, filling the moka pot with water and measuring the grounds.

Daniel stood, grabbing his shirt from the floor and tugging it over his head. He ran a hand through his hair, trying to smooth down the sleep-mussed strands.

"What time did we get back?" he asked, finding his mouth dry. An ache insinuated itself behind his eyes and he fumbled for his duffel. He knew he had paracetamol in there somewhere.

"You don't remember?" Laure's voice was sharp, the sound making him wince. She glared at him as she put the coffee on to boil. "I was wrong yesterday—it should have been you instead of Marcel. How could you, Daniel?"

She pushed past him into the bedroom, closing the door behind her. He heard the lock engage.

Once the espresso percolated, he popped two paracetamol and poured himself a demi-tasse, taking the pot off the heat. Laure still hadn't reappeared. He'd heard her crying, but the sound had tapered off. He'd knocked, but received no response. He downed the espresso and put the cup on the counter before digging through his duffel for his remaining clean clothes. He'd clean up, and if she wouldn't come out, then he'd leave.

The hot water felt good on his aching body, washing away the sweat and grime from the warehouse, from the grass, from the drugs. He regretted it now, what he could remember of the night. Daniel berated himself for his lack of willpower and his loss of control, but even to himself, the words were empty, toothless. He stepped out of the shower and toweled off, wiping the fog from the mirror. His own blue eyes, shadowed and sore, stared back at him, accusing him with the truth.

He was an addict. A couple of months off wouldn't change that. He was trapped. His body conspired against him, the cravings nudging him, first gently, then insistently, reminding him of how good it felt, how much better it was.

Daniel dressed hurriedly, pulling on clean jeans and a long-sleeved black shirt. The scars on his arms seemed to taunt him. Remember how good it was? He pushed a hand through his damp hair, leaning close to the mirror to get it looking half-decent.

When he left the bathroom, Laure had yet to emerge from the bedroom. He knocked lightly at the door, but there was no answer.

"Laure?" he called, putting his ear to the door. He heard a shuffling noise, and leaned back when the door knob turned.

Laure opened the door a crack, her reddened eyes looking up at him. "Just go, Daniel." She licked her lips and sniffled. "I don't want to see you again until you're clean." She shut the door before he could say anything.

He tried the knob, but it was locked. "Laure, I'm sorry."

She didn't reply. He waited, but after several minutes, it became apparent that she wouldn't speak to him, no matter how much he tried.

Daniel gathered up his things and checked the time. He had a couple of hours before he had to meet Royale's messenger—just enough time to get to the city centre and find something to eat. He lingered in the doorway, but the bedroom door stayed closed.

The ride into town seemed interminable. Even with the paracetamol, his head ached. At Bougainville, he joined the others waiting for the next metro. Most businesspeople were at work by now, so he was surrounded by nannies and little kids, and seniors coming down to the city centre from their homes in the suburbs. He stood out, or at least, he thought he did. He wanted to get back to Paris, crawl into bed with Benoît and never come out. A child screeched as the train pulled into the station, and Daniel winced again. Once on board, he found a seat away from the crowd and pulled the envelope with Jean's instructions from his duffel.

11 a.m., Pause Café.

He knew it, but only vaguely, having taken the tram along rue Colbert several times while on his way to a club. He'd never stopped in. He supposed Royale's man would find him.

Daniel rubbed his eyes. Would Valois really have gone to the police? He'd performed in the man's clubs for several years, been invited to lavish performances and dinners, been lauded by Valois and his associates. Valois had helped him after Marcel's death, promising to sort out the situation. Had he seen an opportunity?

Whatever he'd receive from Royale's man would be volatile. He only hoped that he'd make it back to Paris safely. He should have called Royale and Valois on their threats. Stupid. But he needed that job, and he needed to stay out of jail.

Daniel disembarked at Joliette station and headed down the boulevard de la Republique. Just a few blocks, and he'd reach the café. He glanced at his watch. He'd have enough time to eat, if he hurried.

He ordered a sandwich and a café crème from the bar man, and settled into a chair with black plastic weaving. It creaked under his weight. He kept his back to the wall, angled so he could see the doorway. A television blared in the upper left corner, showing sports highlights. He watched it absently for something to do, though he had little interest in the Formula 1 results.

The bar man brought over his sandwich and coffee, tucking the bill under his plate. Daniel dug in, the smell of the roast beef encouraging his appetite. He was hungrier than he expected and finished off the sandwich in minutes. He sat back in his chair and picked up his coffee cup. He'd take his time with the coffee. He checked his watch. Royale's messenger wasn't due for another ten minutes or more, so he had time. He tried to take small, leisurely sips, but the waiting grated on his nerves and he finished before the man arrived. Daniel fidgeted with the cup, turning it this way and that in the saucer.

If he just had a hit, he'd be able to sit calmly. Daniel took a deep breath. Ignore the craving. It pushed back, and no matter how he tried, its voice insinuated itself into Daniel's mind. Just one little sniff or one tiny shot, and the aches in his limbs, the hunger of his body, would disappear.

He was going to drive himself mad.

Daniel pulled out his wallet and laid down enough money for the meal. As he looked up from the bill he saw a man had entered the café and was speaking to the bar man. His dark jeans were nicely snug against his fit buttocks, and his shoes were carefully shined, though he wore no socks. He wore a leather jacket that hung off his lean shoulders, and his dark brown hair was cut short. The man turned, holding a cup of espresso, and his gaze rested on Daniel. He seemed to take it all in, passing judgment in less time than it took him to drink the demi-tasse.

The man walked over, settling into the chair opposite as if he and Daniel were old friends.

And they were—of sorts. It took Daniel a moment, but when the man raised his brows and smiled, Daniel knew him.

"Raoul—I wasn't expecting you." Daniel felt silly for not

recognizing him, but he'd grown a thin beard, and a scar bisected one eyebrow. He was thinner, too, than he had been, looking rangy rather than fit from the front. His cheekbones were more pronounced.

"Wish I could say it was like old times," Raoul said, "but you're lucky the cops are too lazy to care much about Marcel's death. Of course, our friend Valois cares—the prefecture checked all his permits, and he'd let a few slide. Cost him a pretty penny to get it sorted." Raoul shook his head in amusement, cracking a grin.

"You still working at the club?" Daniel didn't want to think of Marcel, turning blue in the bathroom of Valois's pride and joy, La Nuit.

"Half time," Raoul replied. "Your boss Royale is a generous sort, but then, he loves my connections." He winked at Daniel.

"Your connections?"

"You remember my sister, Anne? Her husband's family brought me into the business." Raoul patted his jacket pocket.

"How fortunate." Daniel realized he still fidgeted with the coffee up and he abruptly stilled his hands.

"Still got it bad, n'est pas? Come with me." Raoul rose and downed the rest of his demi-tasse. Daniel rose with him and grabbed his duffel, following Raoul as he headed back to the toilets. Once there, out of the view of the sole bar man and the kitchen, Raoul tugged Daniel into a stall and closed the door. The space was cramped, but Raoul pulled out a tab of heroin, wrapped in foil like Mathieu's had been last night, and opened it carefully.

He put a bit in the hollow of his thumb, like an aged user of snuff would have, and snorted it up his nose.

He held out the foil. "Help yourself, mon ami."

Just a taste. Daniel copied Raoul's method, but took less than half of what Raoul had just inhaled. He felt the rush, but it was muted, just enough to soothe the aches. He leaned against the wall, feeling relaxed, as if he could breathe again.

"Better?" Raoul patted his shoulder. "I have more of that for our friend Royale." From an inner pocket of his jacket he pulled two bricks wrapped and sealed in plastic. Daniel gaped. He'd never seen so much heroin all at once.

"How am I supposed to get that back?"

"Wrap it inside your dirty clothes," Raoul replied. "It's easy." He handed over the drugs and Daniel opened his duffel.

Raoul cracked open the door and peered out. "À bientôt, mon ami. Give my regards to your boss." He slipped out before Daniel could say a word, closing the door behind him. Daniel knelt on the floor and wrapped the drugs in his dirty t-shirts, stowing them at the bottom of the bag and covering them with the jeans he'd worn last night. That would have to do.

CHAPTER 9

Benoît took his laptop with him to a café near Gare de Lyon. He had some time to kill before Daniel arrived, and the café had free wi-fi. He ordered an espresso and began his search, making a list of the clubs they could play if they went over to America. He started a file with names and addresses, and it quickly grew.

He looked up Eric James, and found that the man was exactly who he said he was. He'd been quoted in articles, even in the New York Times, and his website outlined his years of experience. Benoît's heart fluttered. This could be their chance.

Just before four o'clock, he packed up his things and headed into the station to find Daniel. The TGV from Marseille had just pulled in and Benoît strained to see Daniel among the crowd. Finally Benoît spotted him disembarking from one of the cars, his duffel slung over his shoulder. When he reached the concourse, Benoît slipped through the crowd to greet him.

Daniel gave him a hesitant smile and when they embraced, he sank into Benoît's arms so heavily that Benoît nearly staggered under his weight. He pulled back slightly but didn't let go. Daniel's face looked drawn and pale, and he had dark smudges under his eyes.

"Are you all right?" Benoît asked. He'd missed Daniel desperately over the past day and a half, but he hadn't expected him to come back looking so lifeless. Worry set in, nagging fingers that pushed him to find out, and to take Daniel back to his place, make him dinner, and put him to bed early.

Before Daniel, he'd never been domestic. Now look at him.

"I stayed with a friend," Daniel replied. "We went out to a rave—like old times. I should have stayed home."

"But everything's settled?"

"For now," Daniel said.

"Come back home," Benoît said. "I'll make you an omelette and then you can sleep. And I'll tell you my news while we eat."

Daniel raised a brow. "News? Tell me now."

"Later," Benoît said, grinning. "It deserves a celebration. I'll buy a bottle of champagne."

"I'll meet you there," Daniel said. "I need to stop off at my room. I have no clean clothes."

"Don't take too long," Benoît said, reluctant to see Daniel go so soon. He'd just gotten him back. "Are you sure it can't wait? I don't care what you're wearing, anyway." He cupped Daniel's cheek and gave him a gentle kiss. The brush of lips sent a zinging need through him and he couldn't stand that Daniel wasn't coming home with him straight away.

"Trust me, I need clean clothes," Daniel said with a chuckle. "Between the rave and the heat, I've about ruined these. I promise I won't be long."

Jean stood outside the back door of Le Chat Rouge, smoking a cigarette. Daniel saw him glance at his watch.

"About time," he said, flicking his cigarette away and pulling open the door. "Did you get it?"

Daniel followed him into the dark back hallway. "Of course."

Jean led him straight to Royale's office, rapping sharply on the closed door. He heard Royale's voice and Jean pushed open the door.

"Après vous," he said. Daniel stepped around him, taking the duffel from his shoulder. Royale gave him an expectant look as he entered and Daniel dug into the bag, pulling out the bricks one by one and depositing them in front of Royale. The man reached for one, his fleshy fingers closing greedily on the plastic wrap. He pulled a pen knife from his pocket to slit the plastic, peering at the drugs within.

"Good."

Just the one word. Daniel stood there, wondering what would happen next. He tried not to think of how good the heroin would be, or the high it could give him. That he'd carried those bricks this far without trying any…it wore on him.

"You can go," Jean said from behind him. "Don't forget to come in tomorrow evening."

Royale waved a hand, the gold rings glinting, and Daniel retreated. Jean closed the door, leaving Daniel alone in the hall. He turned and headed to his room, taking the creaking stairs two at a time. The sooner he could get away from here, the happier he'd be.

He dumped his dirty clothes on the floor by the bed and took a couple changes of clean clothes from the bureau. In no time at all he was back outside, heading to the metro station at St. Germain-des-Prés. He caught line 4 back up to Montmartre.

Benoît buzzed him up and was waiting in the open door of the studio when he reached the top, breathing heavily. Six floors up, at a run, thanks to the broken elevator, and he still wished he could have gotten there quicker.

"Couldn't wait, could you?" Benoît grinned and pulled Daniel inside, his hands going to Daniel's belt, fumbling with the buckle. Daniel laughed.

"Who can't wait?" he asked. They kissed, tongues tangling, sliding over each other, kissing like they'd been apart for a year.

Daniel opened the buttons on Benoît's shirt, pulling the hem from his jeans and pushing the fabric down off his arms. The shirt fell to the floor. When they broke off the kiss, Daniel was dizzy with need. He shucked his t-shirt as Benoît stripped off his jeans and boxers, letting them pool at his feet. Daniel stepped out of them and then he was nude.

Benoît unbuttoned the waist of his own trousers, stripping them off in a quick motion. They came together, skin against skin, and Daniel forgot his craving when Benoît stroked him, his hand snug around Daniel's cock.

He thought he'd fall, his knees like jelly, but he and Benoît swayed in the entryway. Daniel put a hand against the closed door, trying to brace himself.

Benoît pushed Daniel back, and his shoulders hit the cool plaster. Then Benoît dropped to his knees on the parquet and Daniel clutched at the wall as Benoît took him deep into his hot, wet mouth.

Daniel drew in a shuddering breath, his gaze fixed on Benoît's dark curls, on his lips tight around his cock. Benoît looked up and Daniel was caught in that lustful gaze. When Benoît played his tongue along the underside of his cock, Daniel's breath left him. He was drowning in pleasure and the wall wasn't enough to keep him standing.

Benoît pinned him against the wall, his long-fingered pianist's hands splaying over Daniel's hips, stopping the slide to the floor. He drew back until the head of Daniel's cock rested on his tongue, curling the tip to flick at the frenulum.

"Please—" Daniel's voice broke on the word, his mind going blank. He moaned as Benoît sucked just on the head, slowly, delicately letting his teeth brush over the sensitive flesh. Daniel's hips jerked, but Benoît held him steady, taking his time. Perspiration beaded on his brow and Daniel drew in a deep breath.

Without warning, Benoît took Daniel's cock in deep, and that was all it took. Daniel gasped out a warning and tried to pull away. Benoît's fingers tightened on his hips and Daniel saw stars as he came, Benoît taking him in, every movement, every spasm. He'd never come so hard in his life.

Benoît eased away and Daniel's knees buckled. He slid to the floor in a heap, not caring if the parquet was cold on his ass. Benoît wrapped an arm around him to keep him from sprawling and he rested his forehead on Benoît's warm shoulder.

There in the apartment, naked on the floor next to Benoît, Daniel felt safe, and loved.

"Je t'aime," he said hoarsely.

"Je t'aime," Benoît whispered back.

Marseille wasn't home anymore, Daniel thought. On the floor in this tiny studio apartment, in Benoît's arms—this was home.

Benoît left Daniel sleeping, his expression peaceful as he sprawled in their bed, a stripe of sunlight from a gap in the curtain falling across his chest. He pulled the curtain back, letting in the midday sun.

He wanted to wake Daniel, tell him about the American talent agent, about the offer, but Daniel slept so soundly he didn't have the heart to. Instead he showered and dressed, gathering his wallet and keys before slipping quietly from the apartment. The small boulangerie down the road had fresh pastries and coffee and he ordered two large café crèmes and several pastries and croissants. That should tide them over, at least for a few hours.

Back in the apartment, he could hear the water running. He set the coffee on the counter and took a croissant from the bag, biting into its buttery goodness. Little bits flaked off, but he brushed them from his shirt and took a swig of coffee. When Daniel emerged from the bathroom, towel wrapped around his hips, his gaze went straight to the cup in Benoît's hand.

"You read my mind."

Benoît grinned and motioned to the counter. "Got you one. And a croissant. And a couple other things, too."

Daniel took a deep draught of his coffee and Benoît took the opportunity to admire the interplay of muscles as Daniel stretched, and the way his towel clung to his lean thighs. The desire stirred in him. Last night hadn't been enough.

"What do you want to do today?" he asked, hoping that Daniel would feel the same way he did.

Daniel eyed him, a speculative look crossing his face, the corner of his mouth lifting in an amused smile. Benoît wanted to kiss that mouth.

"What if I wanted to go out?" Daniel asked, the smirk disappearing. Benoît tried to hide his disappointment. Daniel's throaty laugh startled him. "I don't want to go anywhere until we have to work. You should have seen your face!" He sidled up next to Benoît and nudged him with a bare shoulder.

"Get these off," he said, "and I'll finish my coffee. Then we have missed time to catch up on."

Benoît unbuttoned his shirt.

CHAPTER 10

At the break between sets, Jean pulled Daniel aside. He glanced back at Benoît, but he was talking to Patrice. Jean slipped his hand into Daniel's trouser pocket.

"A little bonus from the boss," he said, patting Daniel's pocket before moving away. There was a weight there now, and Daniel casually tucked his hand into his pocket. His fingers met plastic and he felt the edge of a sealed baggie. His heart stuttered. Glancing back at the stage, he retreated to the toilets, locking himself in a stall before he withdrew the bag.

The baggie fit comfortably in the palm of his hand and he stared down at the white powder within. Mon Dieu. He closed his eyes and pressed his lips together. His hand shook and he knew he should flush it, but he couldn't. The craving grabbed him by the throat and he was breathless with the need, the desire.

A solid knock on the door broke his focus and he shoved the bag back into his pocket.

"Daniel? You in there?" It was Serge.

"Coming," he called back. He took a deep breath, feeling some of the tension ease. He'd get rid of the bag later, throw it in a garbage bin on his way home with Benoît. Daniel ran his hands through his hair. He'd be fine. He opened the door.

"You all right?" Benoît asked as they lingered at the bar after their last set. Alain had poured them brandy and Daniel swirled his in the snifter. It wasn't what he really wanted.

"Just tired," he replied. "All that travel has really taken it out of me."

"We should go home then," Benoît said. He tossed back his brandy. "It's late."

Daniel swallowed. "I think I should sleep here," he said. He nudged Benoît. "Someone I know will keep me awake otherwise." His joking tone didn't have any effect on the unhappy expression on Benoît's face. Daniel glanced away, into his drink.

"Don't mind me," Benoît said, slipping an arm over Daniel's shoulder, pulling him close. "I don't like sleeping alone, but I'll manage." His warm breath feathered over Daniel's ear, and Daniel turned his head. Benoît's mouth hovered over his for an instant, then descended in a gentle yet needy kiss.

Daniel kissed him back, tentative in public, but more tentative because he knew he'd lied to the man he loved most of all.

They broke apart, and Benoît grinned. "Lunch tomorrow? Come by the flat?"

"Two o'clock," Daniel confirmed. Benoît slid off his stool and stood.

"I'll see you then. Get plenty of rest, because you won't tomorrow." Benoît gave Daniel another light kiss, then was off. Daniel watched him go, feeling his heart seize. He took up his glass and downed the brandy in a single swallow. The burn of the liquor and its ensuing warmth didn't help the feeling go away. He pushed back from the bar. Only one thing would help. He should never have tried to quit.

He paused on the stairs. He should go back down, toss the baggie into the toilet and deal with the consequences. He took a step down, but he couldn't move further. The heroin in his pocket called to him insistently. Just one more time. He could quiet the craving with a taste and then he'd put it away forever. He would this time. Truly.

Daniel ascended the stairs and went into his room. He locked the door behind him and sank onto the bed. His hand shook as he withdrew the baggie and he set it on the covers. For several minutes he stared at it, then he turned away, rising and stripping off his tuxedo, putting it on its hanger. Maybe if he pretended the drugs weren't there, he'd be okay. He methodically stripped off the rest of his clothes, but the longer he took, the more his hands trembled, and the more his craving grew.

It was inevitable.

He pinched a bit of the powder between his fingers. Just a little. He put it into the hollow of his thumb, then sniffed it up and licked his fingers. A few moments later, he felt the oncoming euphoria, but it seemed weaker than before. He pinched a little more from the baggie to give him a boost.

Daniel slumped back on the bed. His breathing slowed and he felt a glorious lethargy stealing over him. For that moment, everything was perfect.

At two thirty, Benoît tried to call Daniel. He paced the short length of his studio flat, his phone pressed to his ear, but it rang and rang and rang until finally the voice mail picked up. He tried again, and again. Finally, on his fourth attempt, Daniel answered.

"Oui?" His voice sounded raspy, tired, like he'd been sleeping.

"What happened?" Benoît asked, trying to keep from sounding sharp. Daniel mumbled something he couldn't quite hear.

"Asleep. What time is it?"

"Closer to three than two," Benoît replied. "Should I come get you?" He paced to the window, trying to ease some of his tension. Daniel didn't mean to have overslept.

"No, no, I'll meet you at the deli…half an hour?"

"I'll see you then." Benoît ended the call. He grabbed his things, and his clean suit in its dry-cleaning bag, and headed out.

He reached the deli before Daniel and decided to settle into a booth instead of taking a seat on the terrace like he usually would. It gave him room to place the bag, and he could sprawl out in relative comfort. He ordered a coffee and an omelette from the waiter. His stomach growled and he was too hungry to wait.

It wasn't like Daniel to be late. Had going home to Marseille ignited something with an old flame? Was that it? Benoît rubbed his eyes. He was doubting again, and the doubt would ruin him. It had ruined him before, and he'd protected himself ever since. Daniel would have a proper reason. He was just letting his imagination run away on him.

The waiter brought his coffee, and Daniel slid into the booth across from him. He didn't quite look like he'd rolled out of bed, but it was close. His hair was damp, as if he'd run wet hands through it, and his clothes were clean but rumpled. He gave the waiter his order, the same as he always chose.

They clasped hands and some of Benoît's worries settled. It was just another day, him and Daniel.

"Sorry I'm late." Daniel squeezed Benoît's hand, giving him a sheepish smile. "I should have set an alarm."

"Next time I'll set the alarm," Benoît said. "But today I have news that will keep you awake." His voice rose slightly with his excitement, but he held off blurting out his news. This was big, and he wanted Daniel excited.

"You tease." Daniel pulled Benoît forward. "Spill."

Benoît took Eric James's card from his jacket pocket and passed it over. Daniel glanced over it.

"Who is this guy?"

"He said he could get us into the Birdland."

"Mon Dieu." Daniel's eyes went wide. He read the card again, then set it on the table between them, reverently. "He said that?"

"I don't know when exactly, but he's interested. I told him I'd talk to you—he came in on Sunday."

"Call him, Benoît. Just think—the Birdland. Count Basie played there, and—" he listed off artists until Benoît held up a hand.

"And we can add our names to that list." Benoît grinned. "Should I call him now?"

"Did he say how long he'd be in Paris?"

"I can't recall. Why?"

"Maybe he'll come tonight."

"He might. But we can't let on—I don't think Jean would be very happy to find out we're going to abscond."

"Abscond? Like with Jean's family silver?" Daniel chuckled, and the chuckle turned into a full-on laugh. "If only we could."

"Imagine his horror."

"He'd be speechless."

Even the waiter coming with their food didn't quiet their glee.

CHAPTER 11

Jean gave him a knowing glance as Daniel walked into the club that evening, fiddling with his tie. Instead of going by the bar, he turned on his heel and headed to the dressing room, walking calmly. Once inside, he let out a breath. He didn't need it. His hand slid into his trouser pocket of its own volition, but he'd left the baggie in his room, hidden away among his dirty clothes, hopefully where no one would find it.

He should have thrown it away—he could have taken it when he'd gone to meet Benoît this afternoon, but he couldn't bring himself to do it. He'd leave it there and prove that it didn't control him. He was in control, and he didn't need the heroin.

Daniel leaned forward, close to the mirror, and attempted to tie his bow tie. His first attempt was uneven; his second slipped out when he thought he'd done it right; his third he abandoned, sitting down heavily in the vanity's creaky old chair, its burgundy velvet worn thin. Stuffing shifted a little further out a rent in the side. Daniel propped his elbows on the vanity and rested his head in his hands. He could do this.

There was a knock at the door and Benoît strode in, looking perfectly turned out in his dark suit and bow tie. His well-tied bow tie. Daniel watched him in the mirror.

"Ready?" Benoît asked. "I saw Eric James in the audience—this is our chance." His grin nearly split his face, and he squeezed Daniel's shoulders.

Daniel rubbed his eyes and took another deep breath.

"Ça va?" Benoît asked.

"Just nervous," Daniel fibbed. He tugged at one end of his bow tie. "And I can't tie this damn thing to save my life tonight." As if it were that simple.

Benoît quickly tied it for him. "Life saved." He cupped the back of Daniel's neck, leaning down until their foreheads touched. "We can do this, and we'll be brilliant."

"Of course we will." Daniel followed Benoît out and up onto the stage. Patrice and Serge were there, tuned and ready. He stepped up to the microphone and was rewarded with applause. He bowed.

"Bienvenue, mesdames et messieurs," he began. The patter fell easily from his lips, and he focused on tables in turn, some of which held familiar faces, regulars who came to see him perform. He paid special attention to them, complimenting one woman's scarf, hinting to a man that he ought to refill his empty wine carafe, and winking at an older matriarch who sat magnificently at her table, stiff and proper, her white hair carefully styled. This bit of cheek earned him an amused smile, and he grinned back. She'd never spoken to him, but he thought she might now.

Benoît's piano sounded the first notes and the audience fell silent. It was their typical first set, beginning with '*À Paris*' by Yves Montand, then continuing with classics by Brel, Aznavour, Sacha Distel…

They saved requests for their second set, once their audience was liquored and enthusiastic. The old, popular favourites were always a crowd pleaser, a nostalgic interlude from their everyday lives. He didn't want to disappoint.

The last song of this set was always the matriarch's favourite—she'd lean forward slightly in her chair as he began, a soft smile crossing her features, a wistful look as he sang the first lines of '*Hymne d'Amour*'. One day he'd ask her what she thought of when he sang that song.

At the break he descended from the stage and was immediately surrounded by admirers. Benoît patted him on the back as he passed by on his way to the bar. Daniel turned his attention to the young woman at his side. She laid a hand on his arm, rising on her toes to be heard over the chatter of the crowd.

"Je vous adore," she said, a slight blush rising on her cheeks. "Your voice, it makes my heart race."

"Merci, mademoiselle." He bent and kissed her cheek, careful not to allow her too many liberties. She blushed again, deeply, and squeezed his arm before retreating into the crowd. The shy ones were the ones he liked; they never pressed.

After shaking a few hands, he extricated himself, going over to the matriarch's table. She looked up at him with a gentle smile and held out her hand. He clasped it and brought it to his lips.

"Enchantée, madame."

"Bonsoir, monsieur." She introduced herself as Madame Landry and motioned for him to sit. He pulled out a chair next to her and lowered himself into it.

"Are you enjoying the show, madame?"

"Very much. Would you sing something for me? It was my husband's favourite—he used to sing it while he worked in his study, and he sang it when we danced together in the parlour sometimes." She still looked at him, but her gaze was faraway.

"Bien sûr."

"'*Le p'tit mome*'." She smiled wistfully. "He could have given Montand a run for his money, if he'd been interested. But he was more interested in his work, and me."

"If I'd met you then, madame, I would have done the same." Daniel winked and rose. He went to find Benoît at the bar. Alain passed him a glass of water.

"Can we put '*Le p'tit mome*' in the next set? Madame Landry asked for it."

Benoît pulled the setlist from his pocket, along with a pen. He skimmed the titles. "Look to your left," he said quietly. Daniel glanced over. A man sat at a table near the rail, a carafe of wine and a glass in front of him. His tie had been loosened and he looked relaxed. "That's Eric James, the man we've impressed."

Daniel looked more closely. James seemed attentive to the crowd, watching its ebb and flow, turning his head slightly to follow various conversations. Daniel felt fortunate that so many of their regulars had turned up this evening. The enthusiasm ran higher than usual and that could only look good to James's eyes.

"He doesn't miss much," Daniel observed.

"No, he certainly does not." Benoît laid the setlist on the bar. "If we bump the Gainsbourg, we can put 'Le p'tit mome' in its place. Come on, it's almost time to start."

"I'm glad it's one Patrice and Serge know already," Daniel said as they approached the stage.

"Madame Landry will love it."

"And if she sings our praises to Mr. James…"

They ascended the stage and took their places, though Benoît paused to speak with Serge and Patrice. The crowd settled and Daniel scanned over the audience, his gaze resting momentarily on Eric James, who sat forward attentively. Serge began the slow march of the Piaf song they always started with, then Patrice fell into place, then Benoît. Daniel heard his cue. He would wow Eric James, and the journey to America would be his salvation.

When they finished with a flourish, Benoît's gaze was on Daniel, bowing deeply to Madame Landry, who applauded them heartily. Then he acknowledged the rest of the audience in turn, including Eric James, who looked like the cat who ate the canary. James gave him a slight nod, then retreated. Benoît didn't see him leave, but he wanted to shout out the news, to tell Jean and Royale that he'd quit and was off to make his fortune. Instead, he rose from the piano and gave a slight bow to the audience. When the applause had petered out, he followed Daniel from the stage. They were surrounded by admirers, but one by one they trickled away.

Once inside the tiny dressing room, they embraced. Daniel practically vibrated with excitement.

"He loved us," Daniel said gleefully. His strong voice had a slight quaver, as if he couldn't quite believe his own words.

"He'll call soon," Benoît said. "He has my number." He loved seeing Daniel so happy, so energized. "This deserves a celebration."

"The café?" Daniel asked.

Benoît embraced him again, but his hand slid down to cup Daniel's ass in obvious suggestion. "Why waste time at the café?" he said. "I have a bottle of champagne at home, just waiting for us."

"Je t'aime." Daniel kissed him hard and Benoît tamped down the desire that surged in him. He didn't want their lovemaking to be a quick fuck against the vanity.

Breathing hard, they disentangled themselves, straightening their jackets. Benoît pulled on his tie, letting it hang loose around his neck. "On y va."

Outside, Benoît flagged down a taxi. An expense, but worth it tonight. Even the cab driver couldn't go fast enough. Daniel's hand was warm in his and they didn't speak as the cab sped down the Quai Voltaire. Once they arrived in Montmartre, Benoît thrust the fare into the driver's hand and they stumbled out, Daniel reaching into Benoît's pocket for the keys. They took the elevator up the six floors, and Benoît mouthed curses under his breath.

"Patience," Daniel murmured against his hair, his fingers stroking behind Benoît's ear, sending shivers down his spine.

They pushed out of the elevator when it reached the top floor, and then they were inside Benoît's apartment.

Benoît didn't want slow, not now. There would be time for that later. Now, he pulled at his clothes. Daniel helped him, then dropped to his knees. His breath feathered over Benoît's skin and Benoît opened his mouth to object, having wanted to be the one to pleasure Daniel. His objection died in a fevered gasp as Daniel flicked the underside of his cock with his tongue, teasing before taking him in deep.

His fingers tangled in Daniel's hair, urging him on, deeper, closer, until he knew he would lose all control. He tugged Daniel's head back, and Daniel sat back on his heels, his lips glistening with Benoît's arousal.

"Too much?" he asked. When Benoît nodded, Daniel rose to his feet in one smooth movement.

"Not yet." Benoît focused on unbuttoning Daniel's shirt, on slowing his breathing. He wanted to have Daniel crying out his name. He pushed Daniel's shirt off his shoulders, his thumbs tracing his collar bones to rest on his shoulders. Benoît bent forward and placed a kiss over Daniel's heart, his mouth lingering there, feeling the warmth of Daniel's skin, and he thought he felt the flutter of Daniel's heart.

"You are my heart," he whispered against that same flesh.

He flicked out his tongue, tracing a line down his sternum, then over the pectoral to Daniel's nipple, scraping his teeth gently on the already hard bud. Daniel quivered, but kept himself in place. Benoît teased the nub with his tongue, pecking up to sneak a glimpse of his lover.

Daniel had closed his eyes; his lips were parted and his tongue darted out to moisten them.

"Don't stop," Daniel said, and Benoît realized that he'd paused in his ministrations, his mind having pictured what Daniel could do to him with that tongue.

In apology, he trailed kisses over Daniel's chest, laving his other nipple as he'd done the first. He let go of Daniel's shoulders, dropping his hands to undo his trousers. Daniel started to help, but Benoît pushed his hands away. Savouring every moment, he undid the belt, unbuttoned his trousers, pulled down the zipper, then sank to his knees, taking Daniel's clothes with him.

Grasping Daniel's hips, Benoît ran his tongue over the head of his cock, tasting its saltiness, the damp arousal. At the ragged breath above him, he did it again, lingering, letting Daniel rest on his tongue before giving a delicate flick.

"God—Benoît—" Daniel sounded close to begging. His hands came down on Benoît's shoulders and he seemed to be steadying himself. Benoît didn't pause. He sucked the head of Daniel's cock into his mouth, feeling Daniel's fingers bite into his skin. His grip tightened on Daniel's hips as his mouth slowly slid down Daniel's length.

Benoît felt the press of Daniel's stomach on his forehead as Daniel leaned forward, swaying as he struggled to stay upright.

Benoît moved back and Daniel's disappointed moan was music to his ears. He pulled Daniel down and pushed him to his back, making him sprawl to the floor. Benoît knelt between his out-flung legs. Much better. He grasped the base of Daniel's cock and picked up where he'd left off.

The next sound Daniel made was more of a whimper than a moan; he thrust up towards Benoît, who relaxed his throat, taking Daniel in to the very root of his erection.

"I'm—"

Daniel swelled in Benoît's mouth, pulsing against his tongue, and Benoît sucked in his cheeks, making slight movements back and forth with his head. Daniel's entire body tensed. His hot release hit the back of Benoît's throat. He swallowed again and again, until Daniel had collapsed into a boneless puddle on the parquet with one last shudder. Then he gently withdrew, his lips feeling swollen, his jaw muscles aching.

Daniel looked at him through heavy-lidded eyes, his fingers lazily carding through Benoît's hair. "Je t'aime," he said again, his voice thick with desire. "Je t'aime."

Spooned in Daniel's embrace, Benoît luxuriated in the warmth, in the closeness. A melody he couldn't place played in his head with such clarity that he wondered if he was actually sleeping. Daniel pinched his hip.

"You're humming, Benoît," he said, his fingers smoothing the flesh they'd just pinched. "What song is that?"

Benoît rubbed his eyes. "What did it sound like?"

Daniel hummed back the melody. A minor key, notes that held, then fell.

"Once more," Benoît said. Daniel repeated the melody. It was familiar, yet mysterious. He had a niggling sensation that it was a top of the charts pop song from a few years ago, one of those things that emerges from the depths of memory when he least expected it, yet…there was something different.

"I've never heard it before now," Daniel said, pulling Benoît more snugly against him. They fit together like puzzle pieces. "Is it something you've been working on?"

Benoît threw off the covers and groped for the lamp, turning it on. He strode across the room, feeling the chill on his skin as he knelt by the bookshelf, fumbling through a stack of papers until he found what he was looking for—a blank composition book. It had a few half-finished pieces, but he flipped to a clean page.

With an old pencil he sketched in the staffs, then looked up at Daniel. "Hum it again." Daniel sat up in bed, pulling the covers over his lap.

"Now?" He yawned, but obliged.

Benoît scribbled down the notes as fast as he could. Daniel stopped humming, but the melody continued in Benoît's mind, and his pencil raced to keep up.

When he finished, his fingers ached and he was chilled to the bone, but he'd covered several pages. In the half-light the notes seemed elusive, faint on the page, and he wished he had a piano in his flat. He wanted to hear the notes, feel the vibrations in the air, hear if he was right—or if this middle of the night epiphany was a delusion.

Benoît rose stiffly to his feet and padded over to the bed, still clutching the composition book. Daniel took it from him and turned it towards the light, looking carefully at the music.

"I want to hear this," he said, slowly turning the pages.

"There's nothing to play it on," Benoît said. "Tomorrow, we will."

"What about now?" Daniel looked up at him, raising his brows. "No one will be there, and I have a key."

Benoît wondered if he were hearing things. "You have a key to the club?"

"To my room, but also to the back door so I can get in." Daniel nudged him. "Come on. No one will be there."

"You sure?" The last thing Benoît wanted was to run into an irate Jean—and then lose his job before Eric James had offered them a gig. But as he looked again at his score, his fingers itched to play it. He had to know.

"Positive." Daniel glanced at the clock on the bedside table, its numbers glowing faintly. "It's 4 a.m." He thrust the composition book back at Benoît. "If it's good, you can play it tonight, too. Impress Eric James."

They dressed hurriedly, pulling on t-shirts and jeans, pushing their feet into sneakers. Benoît pulled on his jacket, then paused. "The metro isn't running."

"So we'll take a cab. It'll be running by the time we come back." Daniel put on his battered leather jacket and wrapped his grey scarf loosely around his neck. He looked just like he had when Benoît had first seen him in Le Chat Rouge. Hair a little longer, but otherwise the same. Benoît tamped down the desire. Later.

A single taxi loitered at the cab rank, the driver idly smoking a cigarette. Grumbling at being interrupted, he settled back into the driver's seat and turned the light on the top of the cab to red. He sped through the quiet streets and Daniel tipped him a couple of extra euros when they reached the club.

Benoît watched the taxi speed off, back to the boulevard St. Germain. The windows of the club were dark, as were the windows of the rooms above.

"Around the back," Daniel said, taking Benoît's hand. Once inside, they walked on quiet feet to the stage. A light behind the bar had been left on, giving them enough to see by, weaving between the tables.

"Go on—I'll turn on a light," Daniel said, urging Benoît towards the piano. Benoît ascended the stage, the stairs creaking. He heard every sound they made. The feet of the piano bench scraped, and he winced.

He sat in front of the keyboard and laid the composition book on the rack and opened it to his new song. Part of a song. He didn't know what he had, but he would soon hear if his feverish scribblings were as good as he hoped. He rubbed his damp palms on his jeans.

A spotlight came on above him and he squinted against the brightness. Daniel came out of the dark.

"Play it," he urged, leaning against the piano. Benoît laid his hands on the keys, and played.

It was different than it had been in his mind, better somehow, as if the song needed to be made real to show its true beauty. The notes hung in the air, the minor key making them seem ethereal, haunting, but yet not sorrowful. He'd never written anything like this before.

Partway through, he faltered, drawing in a breath when he realized he'd been holding it. Where had this come from, how had he come up with such a thing? The sound faded, swallowed up by the drapery over the windows, the worn velvet banquettes, and the low ceiling of the club.

Benoît looked at Daniel, who blinked and looked back at him. "Was I dreaming?" Benoît asked.

"No," Daniel said, his voice breathless. "Keep playing."

Benoît found his place in the score and continued. When he finished, Daniel came around the piano, sliding onto the bench next to him, hooking an arm over his shoulder.

"Mon Dieu," Benoît whispered.

"It's brilliant," Daniel said. "We need lyrics, and then we'll bring the house down."

He took a piece of paper from the stack by the piano, and the pencil Benoît kept on the rack. The tip hovered over the paper and then he wrote a line, humming to himself under his breath.

Benoît flipped the page back and began playing from the beginning, but softly. Daniel wrote, and struck out a word, and then wrote some more.

Through each repetition of the music, Benoît made changes—adding a note here, lengthening a rest there. He glanced over at Daniel, who had covered the sheet with words.

"I think I might have something," he said, straightening. He placed the lyrics beside Benoît's composition book.

A woman's voice carried through the empty club, followed by a man's. Benoît froze.

A young woman emerged from the back hallway, her dark blonde hair in a loose braid, wearing a dark dress under a leather jacket. Behind her was Jean. He left her waiting by the bar, and as he strode down to the stage, all Benoît could think of was that he'd never seen Jean in any kind of disarray. Tonight, his shirt was rumpled, the top two buttons undone, and his waistcoat hung open.

"Since when have you two been practicing after hours?" His gaze flicked contemptuously from Benoît to Daniel. "And what makes you think you had the right to trespass?"

"I have a key—it's not trespassing," Daniel replied.

"For your own use." Jean crossed his arms. "You'd best be on your way, Benoît."

Benoît gathered up his composition book and Daniel's lyric sheet, but Daniel kept him from rising, laying a hand on his thigh.

"We've done nothing more than you," Daniel said, shooting a look at the woman waiting by the bar. A slight flush reddened Jean's cheek bones.

"What I do is no concern of yours." Jean's tone was icy.

"Let's just go," Benoît muttered to Daniel, who rose when he did. They came down the steps, two against one.

"Before you go, I need to speak to you, Daniel."

"Fine." Daniel put his hands in his pockets.

"I'll wait," Benoît said.

"Go on home," Jean said. "This will take awhile."

"I don't mind."

"If you still want a job, I suggest you leave now," Jean said curtly. "You and he aren't joined at the hip, at least not yet."

"I'll be fine." Daniel stepped in front of Benoît, taking his hand. His body blocked Benoît's view of the glowering maître'd. "I'll set my alarm this time, I promise."

"If you're sure." Benoît took a reluctant step towards the door. Everything in him screamed out to stop, but he quailed inside. Without a definite offer from Eric James, he didn't want to risk his job. He needed the money.

"I'm sure." Daniel squeezed his hand, but didn't kiss him. Benoît wanted to kiss him, but under Jean's gaze, his courage failed him.

"Don't be late." Benoît took another slow step towards the door, then a third. They dropped hands. Another few steps and

Benoît glanced back. Daniel gave him a reassuring nod, but it didn't help. Finally, Benoît steeled his spine and left the club.

CHAPTER 12

"Having a nice romantic interlude?" Jean sneered. Daniel looked pointedly at the woman who still waited by the bar. "Never mind her—she won't meddle. You shouldn't be bringing people here after hours."

"What does it matter?" Daniel kept his hands in his pockets to keep from fidgeting where Jean could see. His fingers ran along the edge of his room key, over and over.

"I shouldn't have to explain why," Jean said. "He's not one of us."

"And I am?"

"Of course you are. Valois assured us of it. We'd never have brought you up here if you weren't. But if you give us away, I'll make sure that you take the fall."

"He doesn't know anything," Daniel said. "I'm not an idiot."

Jean raised a brow. "Benoît believes your good guy routine,

your dedication to your art? He doesn't know your real desire, does he?"

"I can do without it." Daniel pressed his lips together. His fingers clenched around his keys, biting into his skin.

"So you say." Jean nodded to himself, then glanced at his companion, who was starting to look bored. "Don't bring him here again. And if you're going to fidget that much, you can just ask me for your true desire." Daniel sucked in a breath. "Bonne nuit," Jean said. He turned on his heel, taking the three steps up to the bar in one, his arm sliding around the young woman, who cosied up to him.

"Turn the lights off when you're done," Jean called back as he left.

Daniel stood in the empty club. The spotlight gleamed off the piano with its empty bench, pulled out of place. He went up and straightened it, then turned off the spotlight. For a moment, his vision was black, then the faint light from the bar became clearer. He walked through the club and into the hallway. It'd be dawn soon, and his eyes burned from the lack of sleep.

He took the stairs two at a time, then pushed into his room and locked the door behind him. The weak light from the bedside lamp threw shadows over the sheets. It seemed bare and forlorn—lonely. He should be curled up in bed with Benoît, not here. He pulled his t-shirt over his head and shucked his jeans and shoes. He'd manage.

Dawn peeked through the ragged curtain, and still he lay

there unable to sleep. He'd tossed and turned, but he couldn't find a comfortable position, even though his body ached for rest.

Only a little.

It would relax him enough to sleep. When he groped in the pile of dirty clothes, his fingers found the plastic bag. He sat up in bed, the bag in his palm, and turned on the light. There wasn't much left. The craving squeezed his heart, the need rising. And after this was gone, that would be it, and he'd get clean. He would.

Daniel opened the baggie and dipped his fingers in. As if by rote, he placed the powder in the hollow of his thumb and snorted it up without a second thought. The exultation spread through him like a warm wave. His tense muscles relaxed and he slid down to the bed, sprawling over the duvet.

When the feeling began to ebb, he dipped his fingers into the bag again, and came up with the last dusty dregs. One sniff, and it was gone. He cursed and crumpled up the bag, tossing it away. He didn't want to think about what that meant.

Daniel fidgeted so much during lunch that Benoît reached over and laid a hand on his, stilling the movement.

"You all right?" he asked. Daniel had been on time, but he seemed on edge, nervous. "What did Jean say to you?"

Daniel looked away and Benoît's heart rose into his throat. It had to be bad.

"If I do it again, he'll make sure I'm fired," Daniel said.

Benoît frowned. That was par for the course for Jean. Daniel's demeanor had suggested much worse. "That's all?"

"Pretty much. I didn't sleep well, though."

Benoît squeezed his hand. "I don't sleep well without you, either."

"Do you have the music with you? And our lyrics?"

Benoît opened the messenger bag he'd brought and pulled out his composition book. Daniel took out the lyric sheet.

"We could play this tonight, just you and me," he said.

"So soon?" Benoît's confidence wavered. The song was good, better than good, but still he hesitated. It was too new, too personal.

"Why not? Then James can see we're not just content to cover other people's songs. You have talent, and we should show it off." Daniel hummed the first bars, then in a low voice, under his breath, began to sing.

The first phrase flowed smoothly, but the second one jarred, and Daniel stopped, digging into his pocket. Benoît handed him a pen. Daniel scratched out a line and wrote in another, then began again. By the time they had to leave for the club, they'd come up with workable lyrics. Benoît tucked them back into the composition book.

"Should we play it just after the break?" he suggested. "Give Serge and Patrice a few extra minutes?"

Daniel grinned. He'd stopped fidgeting and seemed

relaxed. Benoît liked him this way, happy and eager, the creative juices flowing between them. In a perfect world…

"We'll wow the audience," Daniel said. "And later, we can figure out parts for those two. I'm sure after they hear it, they'll want in."

They paid their bill and caught the metro down to the Left Bank. Once in the club and changed for the evening, Benoît snagged a piece of paper from inside the piano bench and wrote out a clean copy of the lyrics. Daniel leaned against the piano.

"I won't remember them all," he said. "I haven't had enough practice."

Benoît slid them across the piano. "What if you stay where you're standing? We'll come on after the break and it'll look like we're talking—until I start to play. It'll be casual."

"If I were a woman, people would think it romantic," Daniel replied.

"I'll think it romantic," Benoît said, feeling warmth spread over his cheeks.

Daniel leaned forward. "You're so cute when you blush." His lips brushed Benoît's in a tender kiss.

"Didn't you get enough of that earlier?" Jean stood in front of the stage, holding a tray full of lit votive candles. Benoît stiffened.

"What do you care?" Daniel was defiant.

"I don't, but the ladies who fawn over you might," Jean

replied, his voice sharp. "We don't want revenue dropping because you're unattainable, now do we? Monsieur Royale's been impressed with you so far…don't screw it up now."

Jean didn't wait for a reply; he went about his work, placing a glowing votive on every table. Daniel's fingers flexed and clenched. "That asshole," he muttered.

Benoît was sure Jean heard him, as he glanced their way. "Hush. We'll deal with it, remember?" He caught Daniel's gaze and tapped the lyrics. "We'll make an impression."

Daniel took a deep breath. "Vraiment." He smoothed down his jacket, brushing off imaginary lint. Back to fidgeting again, Benoît thought.

"We'll do well," he said, trying to be reassuring.

"I know." Daniel glanced back at the bar. "I'll be back in a moment—I just need some air. It'll keep me from punching Jean." He winked, and Benoît chuckled.

"Go on then. We have ten minutes." He checked his watch. "Make that fifteen."

Daniel left the stage and Benoît turned his attention to the piano. He put his composition book behind some sheet music. No need to let anyone in on their secret. He played a series of chords, warming up his hands and noting where the pitch seemed off. Jean would have to call the tuner soon. Idly, he played a song he'd only heard once or twice, a poignant tune that Sera had performed with Marc Perron. A lover's lament is what it was. He wondered how Sera was doing. She hadn't called lately, and he supposed family, and Marc, must be keeping her occupied. He missed her sometimes, but if she hadn't gone, Daniel wouldn't have come. And he wouldn't give that up for the world.

"Jean!"

Daniel caught up to the maître'd just as he was about to knock on Royale's door. He held a snifter of cognac, Royale's usual drink.

"If you've come to complain, save it," Jean retorted. He looked Daniel over, a slow smile spreading over his face. "Ask what you came to ask."

Daniel hated having to come to Jean, but the craving screamed at him, tugged at his nerves, held his body in thrall. "I need some gear. Do you have anything?"

"I might." Jean pulled a baggie from his pocket, just like the one he'd given Daniel before. "But it'll cost you."

"Take it out of my paycheque," Daniel said. He forced himself to keep from reaching for the heroin. He had to keep some of his dignity intact.

"Done." Jean tossed him the bag. "And there's more where that came from. You'd best hurry—you're on in a few minutes." He knocked on Royale's door and went in.

Daniel clutched the bag tightly in his hand. He opened the back door and went out onto the concrete stoop. He sat down, opening the bag, forcing himself to keep from rushing, to keep from spilling his precious drug.

When the high hit his system, he breathed a sigh of relief. He kept his dose small—he had to make it last. His nerves calmed, his aches faded, and he closed the bag, making it as small as possible, shoving it deep into his trouser pocket. He returned to the club.

Benoît had begun playing while he was gone—his Casablanca medley for the tourists—and Daniel paused at the rail to watch. Benoît made it look so easy, his hands floating over the keys, each touch precise and delicate, his cufflinks glinting in the light, drawing the eye. If only he could stay there all night, watching, being one of the crowd. He recognized the last few bars of the song and bounded up to the stage, reaching the microphone just as Benoît finished his last flourish.

"Mesdames et messieurs, Benoît Grenier!"

The audience, sparse though it was, applauded heartily. Daniel introduced Patrice and Serge, and then himself. "Bienvenue, bonsoir, et on espérons que vous aimerez notre performance ce soir!" He had to stop himself from rambling—the sound of Benoît's piano kept him on track. First, their new song, then a tune from Sinatra, and then Hoagy Carmichael, and finally, into the French chansons. He heard his cue.

CHAPTER 13

Daniel's energy astounded Benoît; he watched him charm the crowd, showing enthusiasm beyond what he'd seen before. He played automatically, his eyes fixed on Daniel. At the close of their last song of the night, the crowd applauded with gusto, and Benoît felt a surge of satisfaction. They were on the top of their game, and he was sure Eric James would call.

As soon as Daniel stepped down from the stage, he faced a deluge of admirers. Benoît skirted them on his way to the bar, but he caught Daniel's eye as he passed and they exchanged a look. Once he was free of the crush, they'd head to the café and a late meal.

Edouard poured him a brandy and slid it across the bar. "Nice going tonight," he said. "Even Jean looked impressed."

"Royale didn't emerge from his cave, did he?"

"That would be a miracle," Edouard replied.

"What would be a miracle?" A young woman with dark auburn hair stepped up to the bar, sliding in next to Benoît.

"I think I'm seeing one right now," Edouard said, grinning. "I didn't think you were coming tonight, cherie."

"Adriana went home early. Headache—or something."

"Something?" Benoît echoed.

"A male something, I'm sure."

"My gain," Edouard replied. "You've just made my evening, Sophie."

Sophie stood on her tiptoes and they kissed. Benoît wanted Daniel, wanted to kiss him like that, but Daniel was still surrounded by admirers. Soon. He used to envy Edouard his Sophie, their obvious affection, but now he had his own. Benoît swirled the brandy in his glass and took a drink.

He was on his second brandy when Daniel finally made it to the bar. "I thought I'd have to stage a rescue mission," he joked. Daniel chuckled.

"It was getting close. Can I get a whiskey, Edouard?"

Benoît felt his phone vibrate. He pulled it out and glanced at the display. An unfamiliar number flashed up; it looked international. He answered, his breath catching in his throat.

"Eric James here. Are you still interested in performing at the Birdland?"

"Yes, of course. Most definitely." Benoît stuttered. He grabbed Daniel's arm.

"We have a full week's booking, two months from now. Do

you have a pen?" Benoît signalled to Edouard for a pen and paper, and the bartender took one from his pocket and tore off a section of paper from his receipts.

"Ready." Benoît jotted down the information as James reeled it off: dates, visas, where to stay, and his email address.

"Get in touch and we'll get the process started. I'll email you the contract tonight."

"Thank you so much." Benoît felt like he was walking on air. James rang off and Benoît stared at his phone as if he couldn't believe it.

Daniel shook him. "Tell me."

Benoît glanced around. "When we get home," he said, giving Daniel a meaningful look. Daniel hooked his arm over Benoît's shoulder, leaning in close.

"It's our big break, isn't it?" he whispered, then kissed him, hard. It was passionate and hot, and Benoît's knees weakened, and he kissed Daniel back. It was their big break. Their chance to get out of here.

Behind them, a man cleared his throat. Benoît broke off the kiss. "You're not in your bedroom, gentlemen," Jean said.

"Let's head out," Daniel said, ignoring Jean. He laid money on the bar for their drinks, then downed his whiskey in one gulp. "À bientôt, Edouard, Sophie."

With his arm still over Benoît's shoulder, they gathered their things and left Le Chat Rouge behind. The night air was welcome after the heat from the crowded club. They caught a cab at the taxi rank on the boulevard.

"We're on our way," Daniel crowed. "New York, the Birdland—it's ours for the taking." They kissed again hungrily.

"We never drank that champagne the other night," Benoît said. "It's still in the fridge."

"We'll drink it tonight," Daniel declared.

When they returned to the flat, he went straight to the fridge, pulling out the bottle. The foil came loose with a quick tear and he unwound the wire wrapping the cork.

"Ready?"

Benoît took out two tumblers from the cupboard. He didn't have champagne flutes.

"That'll do." Daniel popped the cork and it ricocheted off the ceiling, bouncing away to the far corner. He poured quickly, trying to keep from spilling the bubbling liquor. They clicked glasses.

"To us," Benoît said.

"And to New York."

The champagne fizzed on his tongue, crisp and light. He looped his arm around Daniel's waist, feeling his warmth, savouring his scent, his nearness. He gulped down the rest of his champagne and set the glass on the counter. He'd much rather have Daniel, who, seeing the opportunity, dipped his head, brushing his lips over Benoît's, first gently, then harder. Benoît grasped Daniel's lapels, dragging him closer until they felt like one being, pressed together so tightly it seemed their clothes might burn away from the heat.

They fell onto the bed, everything but the kiss a blur. They were skin to skin and Benoît wasn't sure how it had happened. All that mattered was that they were, and he clasped Daniel to him, feeling the flex of muscle, the brush of his legs, the hard press of his cock against Benoît's abdomen, his own urgent hardness.

Daniel's fingers wrapped around Benoît's cock and his heart stuttered and leapt in time with Daniel's strokes. The pleasure overwhelmed him, his back arched, his breath coming in gasps. He flew to the edge of orgasm and teetered there, willing himself not to let go, not yet.

"I want you," Daniel said, his voice a hoarse whisper. He shifted so Benoît lay on his back, using his knee to spread Benoît's legs. He reached over to the night stand and took out a condom and lube. His fingers dipped between Benoît's legs, slick and cool. "Are you ready for me?"

"Always."

Daniel pressed his fingers inside, stroking, working them against Benoît's prostate. Benoît jerked up and Daniel withdrew, winking at him. "Not yet, mon coeur." He sheathed himself, then pushed Benoît's legs wider still. He slide inside in one quick stroke, taking Benoît's breath away.

His thrusts were long, even, letting Benoît get into a rhythm, his body tingling as his arousal grew. Daniel hooked his hands behind Benoît's knees, lifting his legs over his shoulders, opening him up. Benoît grasped Daniel's waist, gripping him tightly, keeping him from withdrawing fully. He wanted Daniel to fill him, lose control in him. He angled his hips and Daniel went deeper still, in to the hilt. He wrapped his legs around Daniel's waist.

"Harder," he gasped. Daniel groaned, his head down, his hair hanging in his eyes. He hunched over Benoît and they were chest to chest, breathing each other's breaths.

"Mon Dieu—Benoît—" Daniel increased his pace, his thrusts becoming erratic. He changed the angle slightly and Benoît moaned.

"Daniel—" Benoît couldn't speak; he came hard, splattering them both with his hot release. Daniel's forehead dropped to Benoît's shoulder and he panted. His whole body seemed to shudder and stiffen, and he gave a low groan as he collapsed onto Benoît.

Benoît wrapped his arms around Daniel, cupping the back of his neck, his thumb stroking the skin behind his ear, a slow, soothing circular motion. He could stay like this forever. After a few minutes, he wasn't sure how long, Daniel finally stirred, pulling out of him and shifting to the side. He rose from the bed.

"Be right back," Daniel murmured, his hand resting briefly on Benoît's chest. The flash of light from the bathroom dazzled Benoît's eyes, then the room was black as the door shut behind Daniel. He groped over the edge of the bed, snagging his briefs and using them to wipe the mess from his stomach. He dropped them to the floor and laid back, listening to the sound of water running, the toilet flushing.

Daniel emerged from the bathroom and Benoît saw his pale, pockmarked skin, the glint of water on his hair, slicked back, in the light from the bathroom. He beckoned to Benoît. "Come have a shower," he said.

"Now?" Benoît felt a lassitude stealing over him, a post-sex torpor.

"Nothing better." Daniel came to the side of the bed, squatting down beside the mattress. Benoît felt fingers skittering up his belly. "Besides, you're all sticky still."

Benoît's abdomen twitched and he squirmed under Daniel's touch.

"Ticklish?" Daniel asked, sounding amused.

"No," Benoît managed to gasp out before biting his lip to stifle the laughter threatening to bubble out. Daniel didn't let up and Benoît curled into a ball, dissolving into a fit of giggles.

"I won't stop until you do," Daniel said, redoubling his efforts. Benoît grasped his wrist but he couldn't pull Daniel away between squirming and gasping laughs.

"All right, all right," Benoît conceded breathlessly. Daniel pulled back and Benoît slowly stretched out on the bed, pushing up to a sitting position. "You jerk."

Daniel laughed and rose to his feet, bending to cup Benoît's cheeks and deposit a gentle kiss on his lips. "I know. Come on." They linked hands and Daniel tugged Benoît to his feet.

CHAPTER 14

Daniel woke early, emerging from a vivid dream, one where he had opened a brick of heroin, like the ones he'd transported for Royale. He'd been just about to sample the wares, and in the dream, his craving had been intense, demanding.

It wasn't just a dream. His body ached and the craving hit him hard. A thin sheen of sweat broke out on his forehead, on his chest, and he took a deep breath, but even that didn't help. Beside him, Benoît slept on, dead to the world. Daniel rolled onto his side away from Benoît, and curled into a ball, his forehead at his knees. The aches intensified and he pressed his lips together. He tried to focus on something else—the light rain pattering on the skylight in the bathroom, the quiet cooing of the pigeons that made their home on the roof, but it only made him more aware of the pain, the need that burned in his flesh.

He slid from the bed, half-crawling to where his trousers lay crumpled on the floor. He dug into the pocket, feeling the bag there, and rose to his feet, taking his trousers into the bathroom, quiet as a mouse. He closed the door as softly as he could, locking it. The trousers dropped to the floor and he held the baggie of heroin in his hand.

Taking only a bit at first, it calmed his nerves, but didn't quench the need. He lowered himself onto the lid of the toilet and took more, then a third pinch, snorting it from the hollow of his thumb. He wiped at his nose.

His hand came away bloody, and he stared at it. Glancing down, he saw the blood splattering on his thighs. He grabbed a handful of toilet paper, trying to stanch the flow. It didn't stop, and he grabbed more tissue.

Benoît knocked on the door. "Daniel?" He knocked again.

Daniel sealed the bag and dropped it on his trousers, kicking them into the corner, out of direct view, covering the bag. He reached over and opened the door, keeping the tissue at his nose with his other hand.

"You ok—" Benoît stared at the blood, his eyes widening. "Jesus." Daniel gathered up a fresh handful of toilet paper and swapped out the bloody tissue for fresh, tossing the soiled bundle in the garbage.

"It looks worse than it is," he said, his voice muffled by his hand and the tissue. He felt lightheaded and the drugs flowed through his system, making it hard for him to stay coherent, to speak without slurring. He fought against the lassitude and euphoria. Benoît would be heartbroken if he knew, and Daniel didn't want to lose him. If he could just get through the next few minutes…

"What happened?" Benoît dampened a towel and wiped up the blood spatters, his touch gentle on Daniel's thighs.

"Happens sometimes," Daniel said. Benoît rinsed the towel in the sink, then came to kneel at Daniel's feet.

"Is it slowing?" he asked, delicately pinching the bridge of Daniel's nose.

"Think so." Daniel groped for more tissue and Benoît helped, taking another length off the toilet roll. Daniel moved the soiled tissue away slowly and Benoît inspected his face, dabbing at the blood.

"It seems to have stopped," Benoît said. He gave Daniel the tissue and stood to wet the towel again. Tilting Daniel's chin up, he cleaned the blood from his face. Daniel closed his eyes.

"Thank you," Daniel said. He held the tissue ready in case the bleeding began again.

"Did you hit your head?" Benoît asked, sounding concerned. He cupped Daniel's cheek and Daniel leaned into the touch, savouring the warmth of Benoît's hand.

"No. Just something that happens."

"From when you did drugs?"

"Oui." Daniel kept his eyes closed. It was the truth, but if he looked at Benoît, he knew Benoît would know he was high. His contracted pupils would prove it. "Sorry."

He heard Benoît sigh, felt his warm breath on his face, then Benoît's lips pressed against his forehead. Daniel dipped his head and opened his eyes, looking down at his knees.

"Come back to bed," Benoît replied. Daniel stood and his

vision narrowed to a pinprick, the darkness rushing in. Benoît caught his arm as he staggered. He grasped the edge of the sink and took a deep breath.

"You're not okay," Benoît said. "Sit down."

"Bed," Daniel replied, hoping he didn't sound as dizzy as he was. Benoît hooked an arm around his waist and they half-walked, half-staggered over to the bed. Daniel flopped back on the mattress and the room spun. He closed his eyes again, biting back a groan. Benoît's hand on his forehead was damp, or was it his forehead that was wet? He didn't know.

"Are you sure you didn't hit your head?" He thought he could hear a tremor in Benoît's voice, but the heroin altered his perceptions, and he couldn't be sure.

"I'm sure," he replied, or at least he thought he did. Footsteps tracked back and forth across the floor. A door creaked—the bathroom door? His head swam.

"What did you take?" Benoît's voice was distant, then close, hands grasping his shoulders, shaking him. "Daniel!"

Daniel cracked his eyes open. Benoît cursed and scrubbed his face with a hand.

"I need to call an ambulance." Benoît rose from the bed and searched for his pants, and his phone.

"No—" Daniel croaked. "No hospitals."

"You need help," Benoît argued. He found his phone, turned it on. Daniel heard the chime.

"I'll be fine." Daniel forced himself to sit up, though his dizziness hadn't subsided. "Don't call." He closed his hand over Benoît's, covering the phone.

Benoît pulled away. "What did you take?"

Daniel didn't answer, and Benoît grabbed his duffel bag from the floor, pawing through it. When he didn't find anything, he dumped it and went through Daniel's jacket. He went into the bathroom and Daniel heard him curse. The floor shook as Benoît stormed back into the main room. Daniel didn't need to look to know what he held.

"When—no, where—did you get this?" Benoît held the baggie with two fingers, as if it were poisonous. Even through the nausea and the pain of disappointing Benoît, Daniel felt the craving kick in again, deep in his belly, clawing at him.

"It doesn't matter." Daniel reached out. "Give it to me."

"Not on your life." Benoît stepped back. Too late, Daniel realized what he was doing. He lunged at Benoît, but Benoît was faster, darting into the bathroom and closing the door. Daniel stumbled and fell to his knees. The toilet flushed and he felt the loss of the heroin like he might the loss of a limb. He sank back on his heels, his arms wrapped around his middle, bending forward until his hair brushed the floor.

It was gone. Flushed like so much waste. He needed it. He couldn't do without it.

The heroin he'd snorted was starting to wear off, and the aches returned, his body tensing. The chill from the parquet seeped into his limbs. What he wouldn't give for another hit. He shuddered.

The door opened and the light from the bathroom spilled across the floor. Bare feet stopped in front of him and then Benoît was on his knees before him, lifting him up into the warmth of his embrace, cradling him like he was a child. Daniel clung to him, his rock in a violent sea.

"It's gone," Benoît whispered. "Why didn't you tell me?"

Daniel shook his head. "I couldn't. I couldn't."

"We'll get through this," Benoît said, sounding determined. He levered them to their feet and they stumbled to the bed, falling across it heavily.

Daniel wept.

That evening at Le Chat Rouge, Benoît watched over Daniel, playing almost by rote as he debated with himself what to do. Daniel had said no doctors, but Benoît wondered if that was a good idea. Daniel could go into rehabilitation, get clean. Except— he doubted Eric James or the Birdland would wait three or four, or even six, months.

He'd have to trust Daniel's word. Maybe once they got to New York, the change in scene would keep him from relapsing.

At the break, Daniel retreated to the dressing room after greeting a few fans. Benoît followed. Inside, Daniel dropped into the chair, his head in his hands. Benoît shut the door behind them and rested his hand on the back of Daniel's neck.

"All right?" he asked, stroking the short, soft hairs at Daniel's nape.

"No," Daniel said from behind his hands. "My head is splitting." He raised his head to look at Benoît, pale, with shadows under his eyes. "I don't know how I'll get through another set, honestly I don't."

"I'll go see if Alain has some paracetamol," Benoît offered. He bent to kiss Daniel's forehead. "Maybe you should get some air."

"I just want to crawl back into bed," Daniel groaned, but got to his feet slowly.

"Go out the front," Benoît said as they left the dressing room. "It's more pleasant than the rubbish bins."

They parted at the bar and Benoît watched Daniel step outside, pausing to say something to Jean, who stood by the door.

Benoît motioned to Alain. "Do you have any paracetamol?"

"In my jacket, in the hall," Alain said as he poured a glass of red wine for a waiting customer. "Headache?"

"Not me, Daniel."

"Go on and grab it," Alain said. "Inside pocket." A waitress came with another drink order. "I'm swamped."

Benoît glanced back at the door, but couldn't see Daniel. He stepped into the back hallway and found Alain's coat hanging from one of the pegs. A small bottle of painkillers was in his inside pocket as he'd said, and Benoît took two. When he came back out to the bar, Alain had poured him a glass of water.

"Find them?"

"Oui, merci." Benoît took the glass with him back to the dressing room. A few minutes later, Daniel returned. He looked slightly less pale, but still not well. "Did the fresh air help?"

"Un peu." Daniel sat down again and picked up the glass. Benoît handed him the paracetamol. "Thank goodness." Daniel swallowed the pills with a big gulp of water.

"Only one more set," Benoît said. "We could cut a song, maybe two, if you think you won't last."

"Maybe one," Daniel replied, taking the face powder from a drawer in the vanity. "Do you think Jean will make a fuss?"

"Doubt it; I'll look at the list and cut his least favourite."

Daniel chuckled. "That should satisfy him. Give me a minute, and I'll be ready."

"Don't be long." Benoît returned to the club and ascended the stage. He glanced at the setlist on his piano and took it over to Serge and Patrice.

"Daniel all right?" Patrice asked, looking up from the cello cradled between his thighs. His dark eyes were concerned.

"He'll be okay—just a bad headache," Benoît said. "I was thinking we could cut the Aznavour from the set, keep things a little shorter. Do you mind?"

"One less song?" Serge shrugged. "No loss." Patrice

crossed it out on their setlist.

"Take him right home tonight," Patrice said, a teasing tone in his voice. "But make sure you two actually sleep."

Benoît's cheeks flamed, though his relationship with Daniel wasn't exactly a secret from the other members of the staff.

"It'll be straight to bed," Daniel remarked, coming up behind Benoît. "You're just jealous."

"You're not my type, I'm afraid," Patrice said with a laugh. "But if you ever want to introduce me to that redhead who fancies you…"

Daniel grinned. He seemed livelier now—the fresh air and painkillers must have helped. "Remind me later and I will." He looked at Benoît. "What's the setlist?"

Benoît handed him the list and he read it quickly before handing it back.

"Good choice. I never much liked that one." He went to the microphone and Benoît returned to his piano. Another hour and he could take Daniel home.

CHAPTER 15

After the performance, Daniel retreated to the dressing room once more, unwilling to mingle with the crowd. In spite of the paracetamol, his head still ached, though less than before. The full body aches were the worst, in the muscles of his legs especially. He slumped back in the chair. His hand found the small lump of the new baggie of heroin in his pocket. Jean had been surprisingly understanding, slipping it to him at the break.

He wished he'd never tried it, never taken it in the first place. Now he was stuck, and he couldn't quiet the need that clawed at his insides. The whispers he'd once felt were gone, replaced by a need that screeched at him and demanded satisfaction.

Time dragged as he waited for Benoît to come in. To silence the screeching, he'd have to be alone, and if Benoît knew— Daniel couldn't bear the thought. He knew Benoît would leave forever. He hadn't said so, but Daniel had seen it before, time and time again. If Benoît left, he couldn't go on, but he couldn't stand the cravings either. There was no other way for it.

Daniel stretched out in the chair, leaning his head against the padded back, and closed his eyes.

He must have dozed, even if only for a few minutes, because Benoît shook him awake. Groggily, Daniel looked up at his lover, whose tie was draped over his neck, the first button of his shirt undone. Handsome, delectable. He wanted to taste that exposed skin, the hollow at the base of his neck.

"Ready to go?" Benoît asked, clasping Daniel's hand. He leaned against the vanity. Daniel shifted in the chair.

"I'll crash here," he said.

"What for?"

"Less of a temptation." Daniel squeezed Benoît's hand. "You look so delicious that we'll never get any sleep if I go home with you."

Daniel rose to his feet, steadying himself on the chair, and pinned Benoît against the vanity. One hand slipped into his hair, the other moved over his lower back and down to cup his ass. Daniel paused, his lips hovering over Benoît's. "I can't get enough of you."

This, at least, was not a lie. He kissed Benoît with all the passion and desire within him, hearing the low groan in Benoît's throat, feeling the press of his erection.

Benoît groped for him, undoing his zipper and sliding his hand inside, stroking Daniel's cock. Daniel's groan matched Benoît's as he thrust his hips forward, putting himself into Benoît's grasp. He broke off the kiss to gulp in a lungful of air. Benoît stroked him to the root and back up, and again. He shuddered.

"If I can't have you in my bed," Benoît murmured in his ear, "then I want you right now."

He jerked Daniel off, knowing well each movement, each touch, that would bring him to completion. In this, Benoît knew him better than he knew himself.

Daniel came hard, bracing himself against the vanity to keep from collapsing. Benoît wrapped an arm around his waist and feathered light kisses over his cheeks and mouth.

"Are you sure you want to sleep?" he teased. Daniel rested his head on Benoît's shoulder, trying to catch his breath, trying to silence the aches and the need that pressed on him. But the drug was in his pocket and he knew that he could be warm and cocooned, feel the release from that pain. Even Benoît couldn't help with that—the physical pain, but also the mental anguish of the mess he'd made of his life, the mess he'd never be free of. Marcel's dead body, lying in a puddle of vomit, spread across his vision. Laure, weeping, then turning him away. Benoît's fear and disappointment. He couldn't change it, couldn't help any of them. And he knew Benoît would leave. Maybe not tonight, but in another day, maybe two, when he realized that he didn't want to spend any more time with a loser like Daniel, a man who would never succeed.

Daniel lifted his head. Benoît stroked his back, up and down, slowly, gently. If nothing existed but the two of them, here and now, he might be able to turn himself into something good, someone good. But it wasn't just them, just this moment in time. Too much existed outside the dressing room door. Daniel straightened and fixed his clothes, watching as Benoît wiped his hands with a tissue.

"I can't leave you unsatisfied," Daniel said, feeling a twinge of guilt—another one—that Benoît seemed to not expect any reciprocation. He ran a hand down the buttons of Benoît's shirt.

Benoît caught his hand, brought it to his lips. "I'm satisfied," he said. "Your face as you came—I'll picture that all night. Now get yourself to bed before you fall over. You look exhausted." He placed a kiss on Daniel's palm, then curled his fingers over the place he'd kissed. Daniel swallowed back his next words. He wanted to tell Benoît everything, but he couldn't.

"Bonne nuit," he said, managing a slight smile.

Benoît walked him to the back hallway, giving him a kiss. "Call me when you wake up."

"I will." Daniel held his breath as he watched Benoît leave the club, sure that he would come back, would call him on his lies. But he didn't.

Daniel went upstairs.

When he returned to his flat, Benoît didn't go to sleep. He felt uneasy about leaving Daniel at Le Chat Rouge, but if he couldn't trust Daniel's word, what sort of relationship would they have? Paranoia, recriminations…everything that had brought his previous relationship to a screaming halt.

He took out his laptop and logged on, hoping that he could connect to one of the open networks that seemed to appear intermittently in the apartment building. Once online, he searched for articles on addiction, and rehabilitation. He found links and phone numbers, jotting them down. Then he read, and read, finding out more than he ever wanted to know about heroin, and cocaine, and drug combinations he hadn't even known existed.

He sat back, staring blankly at the screen, his mind whirling. If Daniel really was still addicted, a few weeks going cold turkey wouldn't be enough. He thought of the Birdland, of being on that famous stage, and knew he didn't want to give that up. It was such a chance for both of them.

He surfed to the Birdland's website and checked out their calendar of performances. On the dates Eric James had emailed to him, there were their names. He could hardly believe it.

Benoît Grenier and Daniel Marceau, straight from the Paris clubs to you.

A sight he'd never thought to see. He closed the laptop, his hands trembling. Tomorrow he'd call Daniel, tell him the news, show him the website. And—Benoît swallowed against a sudden case of nerves—he'd bring up the possibility of counseling, or maybe rehab. Just to help Daniel until they could get to America.

Daniel sprawled on the bed in his boxer shorts, a candle flickering on the night stand, a spoon from the bar beside it, blackened from the flame. His belt was loose around his arm, but he hardly noticed. Pinpricks of blood spattered the duvet, and the syringe he'd used had fallen to the floor.

It didn't matter. Nothing mattered now; he had no worries,

just this feeling of euphoria, of weightlessness. The world contained only him, and this feeling.

He didn't ever want to leave.

When the pain began to intrude, he sat up in bed, groping for the needle on the floor, setting it on the night stand before he picked up the spoon and added a bit of water from the bottle of Vittel he'd swiped from the club on his way upstairs. A large pinch of the heroin went into the liquid and he held it over the candle flame, watching the concoction bubble and cook. He stirred it with the tip of the syringe, trying to keep his hand from shaking and spilling the precious drug.

He took up the liquid into the syringe, careful not to leave even a drop, then set down the spoon. He slumped back on the bed, pulling his belt tight on his arm to make a tourniquet, gripping it in his teeth to keep it taut. He was using his off-hand—he'd never quite mastered it—and it took him several tries to hit a vein, leaving tiny, bloody spots in his skin where he'd failed.

When he hit his target, he pushed the plunger down slowly, wanting to savour the rush, the tingling high that came with the first moments of a hit. It was a larger dose than the last—he needed it to carry him off, keep him from feeling the pain.

This was it. The magic.

His breathing grew shallow and he dropped the belt. The syringe hung from his arm, still in the vein, but Daniel didn't care. He'd found nirvana.

CHAPTER 16

Daniel didn't call. Benoît checked his watch and gathered up the dry-cleaning bag with his suit, and his wallet, phone, and keys. If he didn't hurry, he'd be late to work. He hoped that Daniel had slept the day away. He'd go into Daniel's room, wake him with a kiss, and tease him for being lazy and not phoning.

In the metro he had to squeeze in among the workers heading home to their families, trudging through the tunnel to his connection, dodging people on the stairs at St. Germain-des-Prés.

When he reached Le Chat Rouge, the club was quiet, having just opened for the evening. Edouard manned the bar, dusting the bottles with a rag. Jean lingered nearby, smoking a cigarette, dressed in his usual stiff shirt and waistcoat, one eye on the door.

Daniel was nowhere to be seen.

Benoît went to the dressing room. It was empty, the chair pushed to one side, a pot of powder on the vanity, just as they'd left it last night. He hung up his dry-cleaning and stripped out of his clothes, changing into his suit and tie. He leaned closer to the mirror to tie his bow tie and push his hair off of his forehead. Still Daniel didn't appear.

Serge and Patrice had come in when he returned to the club, and Jean had gravitated to the door, charming a couple who had arrived for an early dinner. Benoît went to the bar.

"Has Daniel been in yet?"

Edouard shrugged. "I haven't seen him. I thought he'd be with you."

Benoît shook his head. He glanced at Jean, who was still occupied, then headed into the back hallway. He could hear Royale coughing in his office, smell the smoke from his cigarettes. He continued up the stairs until he came to the third floor. Several doors ringed the landing and he couldn't hear a sound.

The first door was locked, and the second. He tried the third, and it opened into a small room, its light off, the setting sun filtering in through the dirty window. It smelled musty, sour, like it hadn't been cleaned in a long time.

Daniel lay sprawled on the bed, not moving. Benoît flicked on the light. He saw the blood first, the darkened splotches on the duvet, and on Daniel's bare arms.

"Daniel?"

There was no movement from Daniel, not even a twitch. Benoît rushed to the bed. His gaze fell on the needle still in Daniel's arm, and the makeshift tourniquet. Falling to his knees beside the bed, he shook Daniel by the shoulders, enough to wake him. He didn't wake. His limp form shifted on the bed from Benoît's movements, but that was all.

Benoît felt panic rising, threatening to choke him. He tried to stay calm, tried to tell himself that Daniel wasn't dead, couldn't be dead. He lifted Daniel by the shoulders and his head lolled back. Through a crack in Daniel's eyelids, all Benoît could see were the whites of his eyes. Horrified, he let Daniel slide back onto the bed. His skin was cool but not cold. Benoît stared at Daniel's chest, but if he was breathing, it was so slight as to be undetectable. With a shaking hand, he put two fingers to Daniel's throat, feeling for a pulse.

A faint, slow beating met his search and he let out a breath, feeling the tears burn his eyes, choking against the thickness in his throat. He groped in his pocket for his phone, but it wasn't there. Benoît swore. He'd left it downstairs in the dressing room. He glanced around for Daniel's phone, but didn't see it anywhere. Benoît upended the duffel, spilling clothes onto the floor. He pulled open the drawer of the nightstand, knocking a blackened spoon to the floor, where it clattered against the parquet. Nothing. He didn't want to leave Daniel lying there, but he had to get help, an ambulance, a doctor…

Benoît tore from the room and down the stairs, sliding to a halt by the bar. Edouard stared at him.

"Phone! Now!" Benoît held out his hand. Edouard fumbled in his pocket, digging out his mobile. He passed it over.

"What's wrong?"

Benoît tried to focus on dialing, but his hands shook so that he could barely hold the phone without dropping it.

"Daniel—he's overdosed, upstairs." Benoît tried to hit the numbers. Edouard took the mobile from him, dialing the emergency line.

"What's going on?" Jean came striding over, leaving a pair of goggling customers at the door. Out of the corner of his eye, Benoît saw Serge and Patrice leaving the stage.

"Daniel's overdosed."

Jean swore. "Don't you dare get the cops here. He deserves what he gets."

Benoît stared at Jean. He could hardly believe what he'd heard. "What?"

Jean came around the bar, intent on taking the phone from Edouard. "No authorities. We'll call a cab, take him to hospital."

"He'll never make it!" A thought twigged in Benoît's mind, loud through the panic that fueled him. "Where'd Daniel get the drugs? He didn't have any before."

"Any you think bringing the authorities here, when he has heroin, is going to help him, or us?" Jean turned on Benoît. "We'll get shut down."

Jean's reasoning didn't make sense. Benoît grabbed his arm, shook him. "You'd let a man die?" He saw the answer in Jean's eyes, and another thought struck him. "You gave him the heroin, didn't you?" He hadn't said anything about what kind of drug, but Jean had known.

Jean wrested his arm free. "Get your hands off me." He didn't bother to deny the accusation.

"Connard!" Benoît decked him. Jean's head snapped back and he stumbled, staggering back against the bar before falling to his knees.

"What is going on here?" Royale lumbered out from the back hallway, looking furious, his heavy cheeks flushed.

Edouard had finished his call. "The ambulance is on its way, Benoît," he said. "Go upstairs. I'll watch for them."

"Ambulance?" Royale looked from Benoît to Jean and back again.

"Daniel's overdosed," Edouard said. "Sir."

Royale swore.

"And you're fired," Jean hissed, spitting blood onto the floor, bracing himself against the bar as he stood. His nose bled freely, staining his once pristine shirt.

"You did this?" Royale asked, looking at Benoît.

"And I'd do it again."

"Get your things. You're fired." Royale's pronouncement met Benoît's back, for he'd already started back up the stairs. He could hear Jean's snarls, but not what he said, and Royale's voice in reply. They didn't matter.

He burst into Daniel's room. Daniel had turned his head, and the room stank of vomit. His pillow was soaked with it. Benoît dropped to his knees at Daniel's side, taking his clammy hand. He felt for Daniel's pulse again. It was still there, but as faint as before. He held his hand in front of Daniel's mouth and nose and felt the light tickle of breath.

"Stay with me," he whispered.

He heard heavy footsteps on the stairs, the authoritative voices of the paramedics. He could only hope they weren't too late.

"Benoît?"

The voice roused him from his stupor, and Benoît opened his eyes. He'd slumped back in a chair in the waiting room, his head propped against the wall, and closed his eyes. He must have slept though it felt like he hadn't. He blinked tiredly, his eyes dry and sore.

Edouard stood there, still in his work uniform, looking as out of place in the hospital as Benoît himself did. He held Daniel's duffel in one hand. "I grabbed your clothes from the dressing room, and your phone, as you asked," he said. "And I managed to get into Daniel's room and get his things before Jean had a chance to go through it."

"Merci, Edouard. You're a lifesaver." Benoît stretched, rolling his shoulders. "What time is it?"

"Three o'clock, or thereabouts. I just got off work. How's Daniel?" Edouard sat down in a chair across from Benoît.

"Not well." Benoît didn't want to remember any of it, but he replayed the evening for Edouard. "The paramedics put a tube down his throat, gave him oxygen, tried to stabilize him. I thought he wouldn't make it."

"Has he woken up?"

"In the ambulance, he did. They gave him an injection of something." Benoît grimaced. It had been awful, hearing Daniel's cries, his groans as he was desperately sick, the vomiting so fierce that he'd shook the gurney.

"And now?"

"I don't know. I'm waiting for the doctor to come out, or the nurse, or anyone." He felt helpless, just sitting here, as helpless as he'd felt in the ambulance.

"I'm sure he'll be okay." Edouard stood, resting a hand on Benoît's shoulder, lending him support. "I have to get home. Call me if you need anything."

"Merci." Benoît put his hand over Edouard's for a moment. "Give my best to Sophie."

After Edouard left, Benoît dug through the duffel and took out his phone. No messages. He slid it into his pocket. The muted jangle of a ringtone startled him. He pulled out his phone, but it wasn't his. He dug through Daniel's duffel again and found his phone. It vibrated in his hand and jangled again. Without thinking, he answered it.

"Oui?"

"Daniel?" A woman's voice. He nearly dropped the phone.

"No. Who is this?"

"Laure. Who are you?" the woman, Laure, demanded.

"Benoît, Daniel's boyfriend."

"Can I speak to Daniel?"

Benoît sighed. "He's not here." Such an understatement. There was silence on the end of the line.

"I know it's late, or early, whatever," she said finally, "but I just wanted to talk to him. I feel bad for how things ended between us last time. Did he tell you?" She sounded almost weepy.

"No, he didn't tell me. You were his girlfriend?" Benoît felt a chill, his stomach churned just saying the word.

"We never dated," Laure said. "He told me about you, how he was in love with you."

"Oh." His stomach eased, just barely.

"Can I talk to him?" Laure asked again. "I just need a few minutes. He's my best friend."

"He can't talk. I'm sorry. I haven't seen him since the paramedics brought him into the hospital. I'm still waiting for news."

He heard her indrawn breath. "Will he be all right? What happened?" For the second time that night he relayed the evening's events, and by the end, he could barely speak for the tears and the worry clogging his throat. He could hear Laure sob, then take deep breaths, as if controlling herself.

"I wish I could be there." Her voice was ragged, and she sniffled. "I can't miss work—there's no one to take my place."

"I'll call you when I know anything," Benoît promised. He gave her his number.

"Tell him I'm thinking of him, and that I'm sorry," Laure reiterated.

"I will."

Benoît put Daniel's phone back in the duffel. He took a deep breath, and another, willing himself not to cry.

"Monsieur Grenier?"

A doctor, her dark hair in a bun, wearing a sensible suit under her white coat, looked at him expectantly. He rose.

"Yes?"

"You can see him now. He's stable, but he probably won't be able to say much." She walked down the hall with him. "He'll have a few days here, then once he's doing better, he'll be transferred to a rehabilitation facility."

"And how long will he be there?" Benoît asked. He slung the duffel over his shoulder.

"In cases like his"—she shrugged— "it could be anywhere from a few months to a few years." She paused in front of a door. "I'll give you a few minutes with him, then you really should go home and rest. Don't worry, we'll take care of him." She pushed open the door and waved him through.

Benoît entered hesitantly. Daniel lay under a thin sheet and blue woolen blanket, an IV in his arm, an oxygen tube fixed in his nostrils. Purple bruises marred both arms. He was asleep. Benoît placed the duffel at the foot of the bed and approached.

He sat gingerly on the edge of the bed, picking up Daniel's hand from where it rested on the blanket. His skin still felt cool, but his fingers had lost their bluish cast. Benoît stroked his thumb over the back of Daniel's hand.

"Benoît—" Daniel's voice croaked, and Benoît's gaze went to his face. His blue eyes, those intense blue eyes he loved, were bloodshot and red-rimmed.

"Shh—you'll be okay," Benoît said. Daniel shook his head.

"No," he said. "I'll never—" he coughed, and then gagged. Benoît grabbed the metal bowl on the side table, getting it in place just in time.

Daniel fell back against the pillow, a sheen of sweat on his brow. Benoît put the bowl aside and used a tissue to blot Daniel's forehead and then his lips. Daniel reached shakily for the cup of water resting close by, bringing it to his mouth. The tubes snaking his arm rattled. He drank slowly, then replaced the cup.

"I'll never get better," he said, his voice regaining a bit of strength.

"Of course you will," Benoît retorted. "The doctor said she'd refer you—"

"It never worked before," Daniel interrupted. "I'll always be an addict, Benoît."

"You'll get better," Benoît insisted, gentling his tone. "This is the worst now, but you'll feel better. I'll do whatever I can to help."

Daniel was about to speak, but Benoît continued. "Laure called. She said she's thinking of you and wants you to get better. And she said she was sorry."

Daniel closed his eyes and his lips pressed into a thin line.

A nurse came into the room. "You'll need to leave him to rest now," she said, kindly but firmly.

Benoît rose from the bed, keeping hold of Daniel's hand. He raised it to his lips. "I'll be back later today."

Daniel opened his eyes, looking at him with a bleak expression. "No, just go. You deserve better."

"I'll be back later," Benoît repeated. He gave Daniel's hand a quick squeeze, then placed it gently on the coverlet. The nurse puttered around the room, placing the duffel in the cupboard, straightening things, taking the metal bowl into the bathroom to wash.

"I'll see you later," Benoît emphasized. "And I'll bring you something to read."

Daniel nodded, closing his eyes. Benoît went to the door, lingering, glancing back.

"We'll take good care of him," the nurse said, urging him out. "Don't you worry."

CHAPTER 17

Daniel hunched over the toilet, sweat dripping down his face, his knees aching on the tile, his hand clenched around the steel IV pole. The nausea subsided and he sat back on his haunches, resting his head on his arm. He hated this part of withdrawal, the cramps, the nausea, the sweats and chills, the pain. He wrapped his free arm around himself, trying to keep his abdomen warm and soothe the cramps that flashed through him. When his stomach roiled he bent over the toilet again, gagging, but little came out.

The nurses weren't unsympathetic, but there was little they could do aside from trying to keep him hydrated and fed. Not that it always worked—he'd thrown up most of what he'd eaten since he'd been here. Right now he'd give just about anything for a hit, but the nurses watched him like hawks and he couldn't get more than two steps from his room. And he couldn't call anyone, no one who could smuggle him in some gear.

He sat back again, wiping his mouth with a tissue before flushing the toilet. The pain that had encircled his belly subsided, but he remained kneeling there, knowing it might come back too quickly for him to get far.

"Daniel?"

It was Benoît. Daniel struggled to get to his feet, not wanting Benoît to see him like this, sweat-soaked and praying to the porcelain gods. His legs ached, having gone cold from being in one position on the tile for too long. Benoît peered into the bathroom, then hurried to Daniel's side, hooking his arm under Daniel's shoulder.

"Come on up," he said.

Daniel staggered, only the IV pole and Benoît keeping him upright. "Bed," he said, and he and Benoît did an awkward step-shuffle into the other room. He curled up on his side facing Benoît, who pulled the sheet and blanket over him, tucking him in like he might a child.

Benoît pulled a chair closer to the bed and sat down, reaching for Daniel's hand. Daniel drank in the warmth of Benoît's touch, wishing again that he wasn't in the hospital, that he could crawl into bed with Benoît and never emerge.

"How are you?" Benoît asked, his tone and expression serious, worried.

Daniel tried to smile, to put on a brave face, but his dry lips cracked and it hurt to try. "Been better," he said finally. The setting sun filtered in through the half-closed blinds and he realized he'd been in the bathroom for several hours. He frowned. "Why aren't you at work?"

Benoît ran his free hand through his hair, looking

uncharacteristically sheepish. "I was fired."

"What?" If Daniel had the energy, he would have leapt to his feet and stormed down to Le Chat Rouge. Instead, he squeezed Benoît's hand. "Why would they fire you? I'm the one who caused the trouble."

"I punched out Jean," Benoît admitted. "Probably broke his nose."

Daniel just stared. He'd never thought Benoît would resort to violence.

"I'll find something else," Benoît said. "I don't regret it. That bastard deserved it."

"If it wasn't for me, you'd still have a job."

"If I hadn't met you…" Benoît trailed off, staring into the middle distance, looking pensive.

"You'd be better off," Daniel finished for him. He'd always brought misery to those he loved, and had done it to Benoît, whom he loved most of all. He didn't deserve him, or his love. Daniel's throat tightened and he looked down, away from Benoît, trying to stifle the despair. He should have died, should have followed Marcel into Purgatory. A life for a life. He didn't deserve anything else.

"Daniel." Benoît's warm hand cupped his cheek, his touch gentle, his thumb stroking his cheek bone. Daniel glanced up, and the look in Benoît's eyes—the love, the sorrow—was like a knife in the heart.

"Just go," Daniel said hoarsely, averting his gaze. "Get on

with your life. I'll only drag you down."

"Daniel, I—"

Daniel wrested his hand free and pushed Benoît away with what little strength he possessed. "Go." He didn't dare look at him, at the hurt expression Benoît wore, or at the pity he knew was there also. Benoît's chair scraped against the floor and he saw Benoît's feet as he rose.

"I'll come see you tomorrow," Benoît said, sounding disheartened.

"Don't," Daniel replied, though the pain lanced through his heart. Benoît would be better off. He kept his gaze fixed on the floor.

Benoît didn't speak, though Daniel heard his intake of breath, the sharp sound almost a whimper. The silence stretched out between them, then was broken by the sound of Benoît's footsteps retreating.

Benoît sat heavily on the bench at the bus stop, shaking with the effort to keep from crying out, from cursing Daniel, from going back upstairs to yell and plead. It wouldn't help. Daniel meant what he said. He remembered before, after the first time they'd made love and Daniel had been so sure he'd be rejected. When he hadn't pushed Daniel away then, he'd never expected that Daniel would be the one to push him away instead.

And it hurt. This was why he'd stayed away from relationships. He'd been stupid to try again. He'd known better, but still he'd tried. Never again.

The bus ride home was long and he trudged up the street to his apartment, taking the elevator to the top floor, his energy spent. His phone rang as he closed the door and he answered it without looking at the number, hoping against hope that it was Daniel calling. He'd told himself never again, but he couldn't help it.

"Mr. Grenier." Eric James's American-accented French greeted him. "You need to send me the contract. Have you forgotten?"

"We can't play the Birdland," Benoît said, a dreadful finality to his words. He wanted to take them back, but without Daniel, he didn't want to go to America. The dream was dead.

"I don't understand." James was flabbergasted.

"Mr. Marceau is ill in hospital," Benoît said dully. "He won't be able to make those dates. We might never be able to."

"That's a real shame," James replied. He said a few other things, mostly platitudes, but Benoît didn't pay much attention. He rang off and Benoît set his phone on the night stand before sprawling onto the bed. The tears he'd been holding back since the hospital would not be denied. Not now.

CHAPTER 18

Benoît pushed back from the piano, rising slowly so as not to bump his head on the wooden beam in the middle of the low ceiling. The small crowd applauded and he made a short bow towards them before retreating from the stage, heading into the dressing room.

This club, in the fourth arrondissement, was situated in a cellar, and the walls were stone blocks, as if it had been a wine cave in a previous lifetime. He shivered and buttoned his suit jacket. He wasn't claustrophobic, but he had yet to get used to the small space. He grabbed his jacket and returned to the main room, sliding into the crowd unnoticed.

Pausing at the bar, he shook hands with the owner, an older man who wore a dark suit with a white shirt, open at the collar. His jacket lay unbuttoned over his slight paunch, and his hair receded from his forehead, brown shot through with grey.

"Well done, Grenier," he said. "We'll have you on all week, Tuesday through Friday."

"Merci beaucoup, Laurent." Benoît relaxed. Tonight had been a test, and he'd passed. He wouldn't make as much as he had at Le Chat Rouge, but it would be enough to live on.

"And if it continues to go well, we'll put you in on weekends with Solange, our lovely chanteuse," Laurent replied. "Fabien, give Grenier a drink."

"Brandy, s'il vous plaît," Benoît said to the bartender.

"I'll see you tomorrow," Laurent said. "Fabien, I'll be in my office."

Benoît leaned on the bar. Playing with another singer…it wouldn't be the same. He wished Daniel were here, then pushed the thought away. The nurses had turned him away when he'd tried to visit, though one of them had taken pity on him. She'd told him which facility Daniel would be transferred to.

"He'll be there for three months at least," she'd said. "Give him time, then go see him. He'll come around once he's really free of it."

"Benoît!" A familiar voice called his name, and Edouard and Sophie emerged from the now dwindling crowd. "Did you get the job?" Edouard asked.

"Starting tomorrow," Benoît said, feeling a smile twitching at his lips. He felt like he hadn't smiled in ages.

"That's so great." Sophie hugged him and Edouard clapped him on the back.

"How are things at Le Chat Rouge?" Benoît asked. Edouard grimaced.

"Firing you was the stupidest thing they've ever done," he said. "They brought in this new guy from the south, and found another singer, but they'll need a lot more rehearsal time before they'll be anywhere near as good as you and Daniel."

"Jean's nose healed crooked," Sophie said with a giggle. Then she became serious. "I don't blame you—I would have done the same thing."

Benoît couldn't imagine Sophie, slender and small, ever doing such a thing, but he appreciated the sentiment. "Jean deserved a lot worse than that."

"How's Daniel?" Edouard asked, taking a swig of his pint of beer.

"He won't let me see him," Benoît said. It hurt just saying it, and he stared down into his brandy. "But he's in rehab now, at least."

"He'll come to his senses," Edouard said with a confidence Benoît didn't feel.

"Of course he will." Sophie sounded like she didn't doubt it at all. "He adores you, Benoît."

Edouard cleared his throat when Benoît didn't answer. "Will this place pay you enough? How many nights are you working?"

Benoît told him. "It'll be enough for now, but I'll need to find something for the weekends, or it'll be tight."

"I'll keep my ears open, let you know if I hear anything," Edouard replied.

Benoît nodded his thanks and tossed back the rest of his brandy. He set the glass on the bar.

"Another?" Edouard asked. "It's my round."

"Why not?" Benoît tried out a smile. He would survive, at least for now.

The phone rang as he was getting ready for work, and Benoît scrambled from the bathroom and over to the counter to get it in time. He kept hoping it would be Daniel, but it never was.

"Oui?"

"Benoît, how are you?" The woman's voice was familiar, but it took him a moment to place her.

"Sera?"

"Of course." He could hear her amusement.

"I'm"—he paused—"mostly good."

"Mostly?" He didn't expand, and after an awkward pause, she continued. "I talked to Sophie the other day and she mentioned you'd left Le Chat Rouge."

"It's a long story."

"She said something about how you punched out Jean. I would have loved to see that."

"He deserved it." Benoît told her a shortened version of the tale, and he could almost imagine she was shaking her head at the mess of his life. "What about you and Marc? Still in London?"

"Still here. Things are all right." She sounded reluctant to say anything further, and he wondered if they weren't as good as she pretended. She and Marc loved each other, but love and hate were two sides of the same coin.

"If he's causing you grief, I could come set him straight," Benoît offered, keeping his tone light. "I throw a mean right cross."

Sera made a sound that was very like a snort. "I'll keep that in mind. Sophie also mentioned that your new job doesn't pay as well."

"And not as many hours—only four nights."

"Ever thought of trying London?" Sera asked. "More than a few clubs here seem to be looking for decent musicians."

"I don't know."

"What do you have to lose?"

Benoît sucked in a breath. Going to London would be giving up the hope that he and Daniel could get back together, could put everything behind them. He wasn't ready to do that, not yet. "I'll think about it."

"You have my number," she said. "If you come over, I'll put in a good word, get you some auditions." He heard a voice in the background. "I have to go, Benoît. Call me when you can."

"I will. And I'll let you know if I decide to come over." They said their goodbyes and Benoît hung up. He lowered himself to the bed. It had been over two months since he'd talked to Daniel. They'd have been in America by now, if things had worked out differently. The address for the rehabilitation centre was still in his pocket, just waiting for him to make a decision. He took it out, smoothing the crumpled paper on his thigh.

Tomorrow. He'd give it one more try.

The nurse knocked on Daniel's door. He looked up from his book, a police procedural he'd half-heartedly been reading.

"You have a visitor," she said. Daniel returned to his reading. He didn't want to see anyone. "You need to start interacting again, Daniel. You won't be here forever."

He glanced up at her. "Who is it?"

The nurse smiled and Daniel swore he could see a faint blush steal over her wrinkled cheeks. She was his favourite nurse, more like a grandmother than a health worker. "It's a lovely young man. You really ought to go see him."

Daniel tried to keep his hands steady as he replaced the bookmark between the pages and put the book on the side table. He knew it was Benoît. It couldn't be anyone else.

He'd dreamed of Benoît, night after night, of being in his arms, kissing him, caressing him, curled up in bed together. Some of the dreams were so vivid that he'd been distraught when he awoke and found himself still in his bed at the centre. He wanted to fall into Benoît's embrace, to be loved again, but after what he'd done, he doubted Benoît loved him anymore.

Daniel rose from his chair and the nurse smiled. "Let's get this over with," he said. They walked down the hall, but when Daniel turned to go to the small reception area, she put a hand on his arm.

"I took him into the garden," she said, steering him around. "It's so warm out there today, and you need to get more sun."

"Merci, Simone." Daniel bent and kissed her cheek.

"Go on then," she said. "I'll come for you at dinner."

He headed towards the garden, pushing open the door that led into the small space, the centre courtyard of the complex. Benoît wasn't hard to spot. He sat on a bench beside a lilac bush in full bloom, its tiny purple blossoms spilling everywhere. His dark curls shone in the sun, and he wore a black t-shirt and jeans.

Daniel felt the desire rise and he paused, gathering up his courage. The ache he'd felt from missing Benoît grew more painful, and he pushed forward. When Benoît saw him, he rose from the bench, taking a step forward, his smile reserved and tentative. Daniel stopped in front of him, not knowing what to say, what to do.

Benoît broke through the awkwardness, taking Daniel in an enveloping hug. Daniel clung to him as if he were a life preserver and he was drowning, and Benoît held him tight, just like in his dream. He wanted this moment to last forever.

It was Benoît who stepped back first, though gently, almost apologetically. "Thank you for seeing me," he said. "I was beginning to think you hated me."

"I've never hated you." Daniel sank down onto the bench and Benoît sat next to him. Their hands found each other and Benoît's touch felt like a lifeline.

"You hated yourself." It was a statement without rancor, without judgment. Daniel started to deny it, then stopped.

"Maybe," he admitted. His shoulders drooped and he hung his head. That hadn't changed. Guilt weighed heavily on him; guilt over Marcel, over Laure, and over Benoît, for dragging him into this whole mess.

"If you hadn't seen me today, I would have given up," Benoît said. Daniel's head snapped up. Benoît was smiling and he leaned forward, cupping the back of Daniel's neck. "But I hoped it wouldn't end like that."

"I won't ever go back to the club," Daniel said. "They'd kill me."

Benoît gaped at him.

"Royale's a gangster, Benoît. And Jean's as good as. I knew enough of that sort in Marseille; I might have ended up one myself, if things had turned out differently, if I hadn't been so hooked on drugs."

"Never. Don't you even think it," Benoît said. "But I did think about talking to the police about Jean."

Daniel recoiled. "Don't—please."

"What else happened? Why shouldn't I? Jean was dealing drugs."

Daniel thought of those drugs, the bricks of heroin he'd brought from Marseille. "It's too dangerous. They know how to get away, and they'd leave me to take the fall. Benoît, I need to tell you something about when I went to Marseille."

Benoît looked perplexed. "But I know about Laure," he said. "She told me."

"It's not about Laure." He told his tale, knowing that Benoît would hate him afterwards and that it would end. But it had to come out, and Benoît had to understand who Daniel was.

"Mon Dieu."

Daniel cringed inside; he tried to pull his hand away, but Benoît wouldn't let go.

"I wish you'd told me," Benoît said. "I could have helped you, done something."

"Stood up to Royale? To Jean?" Daniel shook his head. "Then you'd have gotten into trouble with me."

"Maybe not that," Benoît conceded, "but we could have figured out a way, even if it meant quitting. The important thing is that you'd have been safe. And you wouldn't have had to become a drug courier."

Daniel didn't know what to say. He should have trusted Benoît, confided in him. He imagined what it might have been like, how things might have been different.

"What will you do once you're out of rehab?" Benoît asked, breaking the silence. His thumb stroked over Daniel's knuckles.

"I don't know."

"Ever considered London?" Benoît sounded hopeful, eager. Daniel frowned.

"Why London?" He'd imagined leaving Paris, but didn't know where to go. He wouldn't go back to Marseille; it held as much temptation as ever, and the danger was just as high. America was a possibility, and that reminded him. "But what about the Birdland?"

"We'd have been playing there now," Benoît replied, "if it was to be." He gave a shrug when Daniel stammered an apology. Benoît had been hoping for that opportunity, and he knew how much of a disappointment it must have been. "We'll get there, eventually. But what do you think about London? We could find work, make a name for ourselves…"

"You'll go even if I say no, won't you?"

Benoît shifted on the bench, his gaze flitting away. "Not for awhile yet. Sera said she could get me—get us—an audition, but I have a job here in Paris for now. I can wait until you're recovered, if that's what's worrying you."

"You can't rely on me," Daniel said miserably. He wasn't even sure if rehab would work; it hadn't before. He said as much to Benoît.

Benoît sat back, his gaze drifting over the raised flowerbeds, the cobblestone pathway. He seemed to be debating with himself and Daniel dreaded what the decision might be.

"Can you be honest with me?" Benoît asked, his gaze

refocusing on Daniel, intense and serious.

"I can try."

"That's not enough." The words were soft, but they struck a blow nonetheless. Daniel pressed his lips together, not wanting to cry.

"I need to trust you, Daniel. If you can tell me the truth—if you're craving a hit—I won't judge. I won't let you deal with it alone. I can promise you that." He raised Daniel's hand to his lips, pressing a kiss to the back, holding it there for a long moment. "You need to trust me in return. I promise I won't let you down, or let you go it alone."

Daniel stared at Benoît, hardly believing what he'd heard. Not alone. Him and Benoît, wherever they might go, wherever in the world they might be, they'd be together.

"You're sure?" he couldn't help but ask. His voice broke.

"Always." Benoît pulled Daniel into his embrace and they clung to each other. Daniel felt the hot gush of tears on his cheeks and he let them come.

"I promise," he said, his voice muffled as he rested his head on Benoît's shoulder. He felt Benoît's fingers carding through his hair, the touch soothing him like no other.

"Boys!" A cheerful voice broke into their moment of reconciliation, and Daniel raised his head. Simone stood at the garden door. "Dinner in five minutes!" Her smile was contagious and Daniel's lips quirked up. Benoît chuckled, easing his embrace.

"I don't think I've been called a boy since I was about

twelve," he remarked. His voice sounded rough and he swiped at the tears on his own cheeks.

Daniel sat up, using his shirt to wipe his face. "She treats everyone here like her children," he said.

"Boys," they heard her call again. "Daniel, tell your boyfriend he can stay for dinner. We have plenty."

"Shall we?" Benoît pressed a kiss to Daniel's lips. Daniel kissed him back, putting all his pent up desire into the kiss. It had been so long, and he felt like a dying man in the desert would when given water. When they broke apart, they both were breathing hard.

"Let's go," Daniel said. He rose from the bench and reached for Benoît's hand.

They went inside together.

THE END

Read on for an excerpt from **THE PARIS GAME**, the first book in the Le Chat Rouge series, released June 2013, and available in ebook and paperback.

*

On the darker side of Paris, it's dangerous to not pay your debts…

A singer in a jazz club past its prime, Sera Durand must come up with thousands of euros to pay back her boss, a ruthless gangster. A confrontation with her ex, an art dealer profiting on the wrong side of the law, leads her into a questionable wager, but one that could solve her problems.

Marc Perron knows a winning proposition when he sees one. Seducing a shy young woman of Sera's acquaintance will be the easiest thing in the world, and the prize, to have Sera in his bed once again, is worth the chance of losing a sizable sum. What he didn't expect was the depth of Sera's desperation.

When one of his deals goes awry, Marc's solution could cost them more than money…

Sera could hear the murmur of the growing crowd. Friday nights were her favourite; she loved singing for a full house. It made her fantasies of success seem real, and her cut of the cover charge would give her enough to pay Royale for another week. €300. She'd just make it without leaving herself destitute.

A brisk knock at the door announced Benoît's presence.

"Are you ready?"

"Just about." Sera leaned forward, picking up her face powder. "I'll be out in a minute."

Benoît's reflection grinned. "Two minutes," he told her. The door shut behind him.

Sera applied her powder and made the final touches to her makeup. She rose and smoothed down her dress. It clung to her curves and dipped to give her more than a hint of cleavage in front, and left bare an expanse of her pale back. Perfect to impress the crowd, and Jeremy Gordon, if he decided to return. She'd spend the evening with him if she could. She gave herself a once-over in the mirror and put a sultry smile on her face before she opened the door.

She strode out into the club, scanning the crowd for familiar faces as she approached the stage. Benoît held out a hand and helped her up the short stair. Serge and Patrice were already there, talking in low tones. Patrice cradled his cello as he talked, gesturing with the bow as he made some point to Serge. Edouard came to the edge of the stage, holding a glass of water. She bent to take it from him.

"Look for a slim girl with dark auburn hair," she told him.

"Why?"

"Just trust me. You'll like her, I'm sure of it." His aggrieved expression amused her. "You won't regret it, Edouard."

"I'll watch for her," he conceded. "What's her name?"

"Sophie. She's Canadian. And she's an artist—just like you." His expression softened and she thought she saw a hint of a smile. He nodded and headed back to the bar.

She set the water at the side of the stage, tucked behind one of the small speakers. As she stepped up to the microphone, she glanced at the band. Benoît gave her a nod and she heard the opening bars of 'Le Vagabond'.

The first lines came easily and she saw the club's patrons turn their heads to listen. Even Jean paused in his work, holding a snifter of cognac. Her confidence swelled and she allowed a small smile to hover on her lips between verses, widening as she saw Jeremy Gordon moving from the bar to a better vantage point. Perfect. Near him, Sophie waited her turn for a drink. Sera met Edouard's gaze across the bar and knew he'd spotted her as well. She watched them until the song finished and she had to turn her attention back to the band.

Benoît had chosen a song by Dietrich for their next piece, one of her favourites. It seemed appropriate to sing about falling in love again as she watched Sophie hover by the bar with her drink, Edouard speaking to her every time he had a lull in his work. Satisfied, she let her gaze wander.

The flicker of a cigarette lighter in the gloom caught her eye. It flickered again and held, illuminating the face of a man she hadn't seen in weeks. Marc Perron lit his cigarette and his features faded back into the shadows. Not that she needed bright sunlight.

He would be elegantly dressed—a suit, pressed shirts with cufflinks, and depending on his mood, a tie. For all his apparent fastidiousness, he was never a dandy. Even now, moving amongst the crowd to stand at the rail, clear to her gaze, he confidently filled his space. He had a certainty about him, even when they'd first met in that tiny bar years ago. He'd beckoned her over, introduced himself, and had her telling him all her troubles before the night was over. Tonight, he gave her a hungry look that caused her to catch her breath in the midst of the phrase she was singing. She saw that half smile of amusement as he sipped a glass of wine. No one else had noticed her distraction, but he knew.

She pulled herself away, looking anywhere but at him. She found Jeremy Gordon at a table to her left, tucked into a corner, and he looked relaxed, watching her. Sophie had found a small table for two. She'd see Sophie, and then spend time with Jeremy. He might be generous enough to buy her a few drinks, or dinner. That was where she would go at her break, she resolved, and she would ignore Marc completely.

The music drew to a close after several more songs and she bowed briefly to the audience to acknowledge their applause. She glanced at Marc before she could stop herself and he raised his glass to her. She looked away. A hand loomed from the darkness beside the stage and she let the man help her down to the floor. She looked up at him as her eyes adjusted and smiled at Jeremy.

"Bravo, mademoiselle." He bent to kiss her hand.

"Merci. I'm so glad you came."

"So am I." He lowered their linked hands, but didn't let go.

"May I buy you a drink?"

"Afterwards? I promised my friend I'd see her at the break, and there's not much time."

"Later then. I'll come find you." He brushed her cheek with his lips and they parted. Sera wove through the crowd to Sophie's table, where she was greeted with a look of outright hero worship.

"You were incredible!" Sophie clapped her hands together. "I'm so glad I came."

"It's not over yet. There's a half hour break and then we'll do one more set." Sera took the free chair and glanced at Sophie's empty glass. "We should get you another."

"I would have gone, but I thought I'd lose my spot." Sophie leaned forward. "That bartender is so sweet. Do you know him well?"

"Edouard's a great guy," Sera agreed. "He went through a rough spell and I know he'd love your attention."

"He seemed to." Sophie blushed. "I'll try to get back there during the next set." She craned her neck to glance at the bar. "He's too busy now."

"Things will slow down during the second set." Sera moistened her dry lips and wished she had her glass of water with her, but she'd left it onstage.

"Looking for this?" A familiar hand set a glass of water in front of her. She would have known his hand anywhere, even without the silver cufflinks that glinted against his dark pinstriped jacket. That hand had bruised her, caressed her, comforted her, and had brought her to screaming orgasm more times than she could remember.

"Ma chère, you were lovely as always," Marc continued, the low tenor of his voice husky with intimacy. "If I wasn't away so often, I'd be here every night."

Sera lifted her face as Marc bent and kissed her cheeks, lingering far longer than strictly necessary. She inhaled the subtle scent of his cologne before he straightened.

"Merci, Marc. Won't you join us?"

He appropriated an empty chair from a nearby table, settling between her and Sophie. "Aren't you going to introduce us?" His gaze rested on Sophie, who shifted in her chair under the unexpected attention.

"Of course." She felt a sharp pang of jealousy and gave Marc a terse look. "Sophie, this is my friend Marc Perron. Marc, Sophie."

"Enchantée, mademoiselle Sophie." Marc held out his hand. Sophie hesitated, but finally placed her hand in his. Sera watched him lift Sophie's hand to his lips. Sophie blushed furiously and as soon as she could, she took her hand back, clasping it under the table.

"Bonsoir, monsieur," she replied politely.

"Where have you been?" Sera drew his attention away from Sophie, who glanced towards the bar again.

"Here and there. I was in Amsterdam last week and Florence the week before. And I had a quick jaunt to London for a few meetings. One of my clients was desperate for an altarpiece."

"Isn't that illegal?" Sophie asked, her eyes wide.

Marc smiled at her. "He saw sense and paid me to go looking for replicas for him, or for an artist who could paint in the old style."

"Marc deals in art and antiques," Sera remarked to Sophie. "His family's firm has been around for a long time."

"A hundred years or thereabouts." Marc lit a cigarette, offering the slim case to Sophie, and perfunctorily to Sera, giving her a wink as he held it out. He knew she didn't smoke, but he had noticed her response to his attention to Sophie.

"No thank you," Sophie replied. Marc slipped the case back into his jacket pocket.

"Amsterdam wasn't as worthwhile," he remarked. "The items at auction were poor; much worse than I'd expected."

"So it was a wasted trip?" Sera sipped her water.

"Not entirely." He gave her a look that left no doubts as to what he was referring. Of course he'd entertain one or several women during his stay. Sophie's attention had drifted again and she was glad Sophie had missed Marc's lewd look.

"Have you traveled much, mademoiselle?" Marc inquired, bringing Sophie's gaze back to the table.

"I wish." She gave him a rueful smile. "I barely could afford to come here."

"And what has brought you to our lovely city?"

Sera watched Marc shift closer to Sophie, intent on his new conquest. This was not what she had intended when she'd invited Sophie tonight. She felt a hand on her shoulder and turned.

"It's time." It was Benoît. Patrice and Serge were already waiting on stage. As she rose, she knew how to interrupt Marc's flirtation. It would serve him right and give Sophie a chance to go see Edouard. And, though Sera didn't want to admit it, he would spend more time with her instead.

"Would you play a song with me, Marc?" She turned to Benoît. "If Patrice doesn't mind lending his cello, of course."

"I'm sure he'll be fine with it." Benoît ambled back to the stage where he had a word with Patrice.

"You play the cello?" Sophie asked.

"Not professionally." Marc stubbed out his cigarette. "Bien sûr, ma chère; I would love to. Save my seat, Sophie."

Patrice gave up his seat for Marc, who settled the cello between his knees. He played a few experimental chords and then tightened two strings minutely. "What shall we play?

Sera already knew. She had thought of it when she'd first seen him.

"Do you remember 'Ma Chanteuse'?" She saw a reaction in his eyes, the slight tenseness of his form, but it disappeared before she could be certain.

"I wrote it for you. How could I forget, ma chère?"

The first few notes slid into the club and the crowd quieted. He played through the haunting introduction and Sera stepped up to the microphone.

You walked in and captured the impossible smile...

She hadn't sung the song in years, but she hadn't forgotten the words. She glanced back at Marc. His head lifted and he seemed to see right into her. Her chest felt tight and tears pricked the back of her eyes. She looked away, trying to focus on the music. Her voice rose and fell with the melody of the cello. The audience faded from her awareness and she and the music were in a world all their own.

As she sang the last line, she turned to watch Marc draw his bow across the strings for the final bar. The notes carried in the silent crowd. When he finished, they were immersed in applause. She barely registered Patrice returning to his spot, but suddenly Marc was beside her, giving a brief bow to the audience.

"Beautiful as always, ma chère," he told her, giving her an affectionate smile before stepping down from the stage. She watched him resume his position next to Sophie, who looked at him with some of the same awe she had given to Sera. She glanced at Edouard, but he was busy behind the bar. She'd done what she'd tried to avoid—Marc had Sophie's full attention.

Benoît's piano resonated with the final dramatic chords of 'La Vie En Rose' and then he and the rest of the band rose to take their bows. Sera joined them, coming back to earth from her musical highs. She spotted Jeremy Gordon patiently nursing a bourbon near the bar, but a glance at Sophie decided her. Jeremy could wait. Sophie laughed at something Marc had said, and he leaned closer.

"You didn't save me any wine," Sera remarked as she pulled out her chair and sat across from Sophie. The carafe on the table was empty and only Sophie's glass held any liquor.

"That's easily remedied, ma chère."

Before Marc could gesture for a waiter, Sera looked directly at Sophie. "Could you go ask Edouard for another carafe, and a glass?" She gave Sophie a conspiratorial wink and Sophie grinned.

"Of course."

Marc watched her go. "Was that really necessary?"

"I didn't invite her here so you could seduce her."

"That would have been a fortunate side effect." He lit a cigarette. "Why does it matter?"

"She's already interested in someone else." At the bar, Sophie smiled up at Edouard, standing on her tiptoes to be heard over the crowd.

"Is that all?"

Sera couldn't say more. Sophie came back to the table, Edouard in tow, carrying a fresh carafe of wine and a glass.

"You outdid yourself tonight, Sera." Edouard set the glass in front of her and poured from the carafe. "And you also, Monsieur Perron. Jean told me that he wished you would play more often."

Marc chuckled. "I'm sure he does, but he couldn't afford my rates." Sophie laughed, but her attention was still focused on

Edouard.

"Didn't I tell you she was fantastic?" Sera wasn't sure that Edouard's grin could get any wider.

"You were right," Sophie replied, her cheeks flushed. Not from shyness, Sera thought. The pair seemed to have forgotten that anyone else was in the room. "I never doubted you."

"And now that you know, you'll have to come back again," Edouard replied, gazing down at her. He finished filling Marc's glass and set the carafe on the table, removing the empty one. He seemed reluctant to leave, but finally stepped away. "I have to get back. See you later?"

"Of course," Sophie told him.

Sera glanced at Marc and found him watching her instead of Sophie and Edouard. He gave her a wicked grin as Edouard departed and turned his attention back to Sophie. "Did you know, mademoiselle, that Picasso and Dora Marr used to drink in this very club?"

"Really?" Sophie looked around the club with a new curiosity.

"It's been an artists' favourite for decades. Everyone who was anyone has been here."

"Even Canadian artists?"

Marc shrugged. "Very likely. Is that your area of study?"

"I'm focusing on Canadian artists that came to Paris to study, especially Paul Peel."

"I'm familiar with his work," Marc said. "At an auction in Montreal one of his studies for After the Bath was in a lot up for bid."

"Did you buy it?" Sophie leaned forward, resting her arms on the table.

"My clients were looking for other works. That one went to a museum, if I recall."

"You have a good memory," Sera remarked. The corner of Marc's mouth quirked up in a smile.

"I do."

Sophie looked dreamy. "I'd love to own The Venetian Bather. It's my favourite."

"I've seen it at the National Gallery."

Sophie smiled at Marc. "Me too. I went all the time when I was at home."

Sera listened to their conversation, becoming increasingly irritated and bored. Marc took every new woman as a challenge, and though she liked Sophie, she was jealous. She made her tone sound amused as she rebuked them. "You two aren't being very kind to someone who has no idea what you're talking about."

"The Venetian Bather is a painting of a young girl standing nude before a mirror. She has a towel, and it's done in almost a Pre-Raphaelite style."

"And there's a small kitten chasing the frayed hem of the towel," Sophie added. "I love that little detail."

"You're fortunate to be able to see it so often," Sera said.

"I'd love to own it so I could see it every day, but that's impossible."

"Nothing's impossible." Marc said, his lips curving into an amused smile.

"That is." She thought for a moment. "Unless I won the lottery, I guess."

"If you were really wealthy you could just pay someone to steal it for you." Marc lit a cigarette, taking a long drag. "Money opens a lot of doors."

"Only to become a criminal," Sera interjected.

"As if that ever happens," Sophie said to Marc. "Theft-to-order? Really?"

"I have heard of it. There are more than a few stories that circulate the auction houses." He glanced at Sera. "Another drink?"

Sera shrugged. Sophie looked at her watch. "Just a cab home for me, I'm afraid."

"You need to give me your number before you go," Sera told her. "Marc, do you have a pen?"

He pulled a pen from his inner jacket pocket. Sera took a napkin from the table and wrote her phone number. Sophie wrote hers, and Sera tore the napkin in half.

"Maybe we could meet for coffee next week?" Sophie suggested. She rose.

"Of course. Just call." Sera gave Sophie a hug. "Bonne nuit."

"A shame you have to leave so early." Marc rose and bent to kiss Sophie's cheeks. She became flustered and stepped back. "Bonne nuit, mademoiselle." Sera raised a brow. He certainly hadn't held back.

Sophie walked up the steps, turned to give them a wave and then disappeared into the crowd. Sera hoped that Sophie would stop to say goodnight to Edouard on her way out. She had a feeling she would. It would serve Marc right if Sophie completely dismissed his advances.

Marc turned to her as they seated themselves again. "She's such an innocent," he said. Sera gave him a sharp look.

"She's not your type."

"Of course she is. They all are." He took one last drag on his cigarette before stubbing it out. "It wouldn't take much."

"Just leave her be, Marc." Sera glanced towards the bar and saw Sophie and Edouard talking. "She's interested in someone else."

Marc followed her gaze. "She could do better than Edouard. Someone with more experience."

"There's such a thing as too much experience. And besides, weren't you seeing Jeanne?"

"Not for weeks now. Too dull." He leaned closer. "You would have loved the girl I met in London. She wasn't as innocent as Sophie, but very close. And so beautifully willing." He grinned.

"But only worth a night?"

"She was worth a second night, and I'd be tempted to see her on my next trip as well."

"That's quite unlike you."

He gave her a knowing look. "I doubt it'll be anything serious."

Sera took a sip of her wine.

"So tell me," Marc continued, "Where did you find our Sophie?"

"Our Sophie?" She shook her head, wanting to kick him for his possessiveness. Sophie wasn't his, or hers. "I came out of St.-Germain-des-près and she was sketching the Deux Magots."

"What a shame I didn't meet her first." Marc poured them more wine, emptying the carafe.

"You'd have scared her away."

"I didn't scare you away when we first met."

"That was then. She's smarter than I was. And I don't think you'd be able to seduce her."

"That sounds like a challenge, ma chère."

"It wasn't meant to be one."

She'd seen how Sophie had looked at Edouard, and she recognized the stirrings of first love. She had felt them herself once, and as she looked at Marc, lighting another cigarette, she had never managed to get over them.

He leaned back in his chair, one leg stretched out, his jacket fallen open. Sera knew he was teasing her, giving her something to look at. His trousers clung in all the right spots, highlighting the muscled line of his leg. Her eyes followed it upward, but he interrupted her perusal.

"How could she resist?" Marc caught her gaze. "You can't."

"No harm in looking," she replied. "I'm not interested. And, I have someone else." He smirked. "In fact, he's sitting over there." She gave a slight nod towards Jeremy Gordon, though she wondered how long he would wait.

"Impressive," Marc said. "How long have you known him?"

"A little while."

"As long as we've known Sophie?"

"Longer." Barely.

"And as easy to seduce. He's been looking at you all evening." Marc looked amused.

"Sophie's not interested in you."

He chuckled. "So you keep saying. Let me offer you a wager then, ma chère, since you seem so certain." He ran a hand down her bare arm and she tried to keep from reacting. Goose bumps rose on her skin and she hoped he hadn't noticed. "It's been so long since our last one."

"And that turned out so well for me," she said dryly. "Why would I want to?"

"I'd give you the choice of terms," Marc offered.

"Anything?" She tried to think of something appropriately damning and to get him back for having lost their last wager. She didn't want to spend 24 hours on her hands and knees again.

"Whatever you like, ma chère." He was so easily confident that he would succeed. She wanted to wipe the smirk off of his face.

"Your wager is nothing without a time limit. I'll give you a week, starting tomorrow."

"What am I, a miracle worker? That's hardly fair."

"Who said this was fair?"

"I'm barely in Paris this month. Four weeks," he countered.

"Fine—two weeks."

"Not enough. Three."

Sera took a sip of her wine and tried not to smile. She knew what she wanted to wager. "I'll give you your three weeks, but..." and she paused to make sure she had Marc's full attention, "...if you lose, you'll pay off my debts and give me enough to live on for half a year."

Marc scoffed. "That's excessive."

"So is three weeks. It makes me think that you don't have much confidence in your abilities."

"D'accord. But if you lose, ma chère, you're mine for those six months."

"Yours how?" The wine was hard to swallow against the sudden tightening of her throat.

"For whatever I wish. You'd be bound to do what I required. I might make you clean my flat every day, or take dictation. I could use someone for when the receptionist at the firm is ill." He became serious. "Or you could be tied to my bed for hours to serve my pleasure." He gave her a keen look. "Do you agree?"

She stilled, not daring to take another sip of her wine. She could imagine it all too easily, but she wanted something more than just pleasure. "To become your indentured servant? No."

"I'd still pay your six months living expenses," he said. "I'd just be getting something for my money. And I might even pay your debts."

"Six months is too long."

"So make it three. With the appropriate reduction in your living expenses."

Three months. She thought about how Sophie and Edouard had looked together, and weighed her chances of winning. Marc was a nearly unstoppable force when it came to women, but he'd have a strong rival in Edouard, along with Sophie's accompanying reluctance. She took a deep breath.

"Oui, d'accord." She held out her hand. He took it, but instead of shaking on their wager, he pulled her forward until they were inches apart. His hand cupped her cheek and she had to stop herself from leaning into his touch.

"We should seal this wager with something a bit more substantial, don't you think, ma chère?" She met his gaze. There was something in his eyes that was more than just desire. He leaned forward that last inch and kissed her. She stiffened, but only for a moment. His lips teased hers, familiar and captivating. What would it hurt? She responded to his kiss and he took it deeper, conquering her mouth. If she'd been standing, her knees would have given out. She pressed forward, and when he broke off the kiss, she felt cheated. "But that's not all. It's been too long since we've played. I've missed you. On y va?"

Had he really missed her? She could still feel the imprint of his lips. She shouldn't, but if it were only one night, she could fulfill her desire without getting attached. "Only tonight."

"Until I win," he said, giving her that amused half smile again. He rose, laying a few bills on the table to cover their tab. She let him escort her from the club, ignoring the stares from Jean and Edouard as they left. Marc kept a hand on the small of her back as they walked towards the boulevard to the cab rank.

There were a handful of people in front of them, and Jeremy Gordon stared at her from the front of the line. Jeremy! She'd forgotten him entirely once Marc had touched her. She opened her mouth to say something, but nothing came out. He gave her a wry smile, and to her surprise, got in a cab without even attempting to speak to her. She looked away, disappointed, but only for a moment. Marc slid his hand down her back and up under her shawl, caressing her bare skin. Only tonight, she repeated to herself, even as Marc's touch sent shivers up her spine.

The cab ride was quicker than she remembered, and soon Sera followed Marc up the stairs to his second floor apartment. Her high heels echoed on the marble, slightly concave from the thousands of feet that had climbed the stairs over the years. The stillness of the late hour amplified the sound and even the turning of the bolt carried in the quiet.

She had not gone home with Marc in months, but his apartment was as familiar to her as her own. In earlier years she had spent many hours working her way through the massive collection of books that lined the hallway. Each shelf was organized in its own fashion, but Sera had never been able to figure out its logic. She suspected that their places moved according to his whim. Tonight, however, she barely gave the books a glance.

Marc had gone on ahead of her but she knew he would soon emerge from the bedroom. The living room was as she'd remembered it—oddly modern for such an old building. The classical plaster ceiling moldings were pristine; their pale paint glowed in the low light from a lamp perched on a slender side table. She moved across the room to one of the long windows, stepping around a low leather armchair. The latch on the window gave easily and she pushed it open. The night air rushed in.

"It's very tempting to take you right here." Marc's hand slid into her dress, pushing the strap off one shoulder. If anyone had looked up just then, they would have seen the barest flash of her breast before he covered it with his hand, pulling her back against him.

"But what would the neighbors think?" He laughed at her quip as he turned her around. He slid the remaining strap of her dress from her shoulder and it fell in a dark puddle at her feet.

"They don't matter. It's been too long." His touch on her skin was gentle and she watched him trace the line of her hips and up over her breasts. It reminded her of the first time, when he'd learned her body by touch. "You know what I need." He lifted her chin and his mouth came down hard on hers, demanding her surrender. She wanted it all tonight. She closed her eyes and kissed him back, rising on her toes. She had missed him, even if she'd pretended otherwise. His fingers tangled painfully in her hair.

He drew back from her and let her take a gasping breath before he strode towards the bedroom, dragging her along with him. He brought her to the foot of his bed, where a set of handcuffs dangled from the iron rail. He let go of her hair to fasten the cuffs around her wrists. He pulled the hair away from her eyes and plaited it into an untidy braid. The gesture seemed kind, but she knew that he preferred to see her face when he was fucking her.

"Those stockings are a nice touch," he remarked. "I wasn't expecting them. I hope you don't want them to last the evening."

Sera couldn't help but smile. "If I'd known you were coming, I wouldn't have worn them."

"Did you miss me while I was gone?" He caressed her cheek. She looked down at her hands, not wanting him to see the answer in her eyes. "Did you?" When she didn't look up at him, the caress ended in a pinch to her nipple that made her flinch.

"Yes." She hated admitting it. All those weeks she'd had to try and forget him were fading. All she could think about was him.

"And how long has it been, ma chère? Remind me." He lifted her chin so she couldn't look away.

To her shame, she knew. "Sixteen weeks." Her voice was barely a whisper, but he heard her.

"I'll have to make up for neglecting you for so long." Marc bent her over the rail. He stripped her of her underwear and stockings. She heard the rustle of cloth and glanced up to see Marc removing his suit jacket, hanging it in the wardrobe. She felt like a voyeur, laying there as he unbuttoned his shirt. While he removed his cufflinks she imagined tugging off his shirt and running her hands down his nearly hairless chest. The urge to touch him was so strong her hands moved involuntarily, rattling the steel against the rail. Marc looked up.

"Restless?" He shrugged off his shirt and tossed it aside, coming back to the bed in just his pinstriped trousers. She nodded. He parted her thighs, pressing two fingers inside her. She pushed back against his hand, letting out a satisfied moan. He added a third finger and she wanted to sob. She had missed this. He had such familiarity with her body and it was too easy to submit to a man that could bring her to orgasm in a dozen ways. Marc curled his fingers inside her and rubbed across her clit with his thumb and she came with an intensity that surprised even her.

"You have missed me, Seraphina." She could hear the satisfaction in his voice.

His hands spread her open, and she felt his breath on her back, and then lower. His tongue delved into her. She squirmed to get closer but he held her fast, pressing her hips into the rail. She knew she would have bruises in the morning, but it didn't matter. His tongue rasped against her clit and he took her in his mouth. Whenever he took her like this it never took long before she was on the edge, and he knew that. She tried to think of something else—anything else—but it didn't work.

"S'il vous plaît?" He paused, and she caught her breath. "May I?"

"Oui, Seraphina. You may." He resumed his attentions and she spasmed against him, feeling the wetness soak into the duvet.

Sera sprawled limply against the bed, her legs dangling over the rail. He moved her onto her side and she felt the handcuffs slide from her wrists. Gentle, again. She watched him strip off his trousers. She sat up and reached for him, but he caught her hand before she could touch him. She looked up at him beseechingly and finally he pointed to the floor. Sera knew what he wanted. She let herself slide to the floor at his feet, ending up on her hands and knees on the cool parquet. She rested her forehead briefly on the arch of his foot and let her body relax before her fingers circled his ankles and she began kissing a slow path up his legs. By the time her cheek brushed his cock, he was hard, and his hands in her hair indicated his impatience. She took him into her mouth, remembering just how he liked it—varied—and she never had to fear that she was being too rough. She let her teeth graze the underside and his answering groan was her reward.

Marc pulled her back before she would have finished. He lifted her to her feet and scooped her up in his arms, where she luxuriated for a short moment with a contented sigh.

"We're not done yet, ma chère."

"Good," she told him, her voice faint and dreamy. He chuckled and lowered her to the bed. Sera leaned back against the pillows and watched as he took a wrapped condom and lubrication from the drawer of the night stand. She hadn't forgotten what that meant. She crawled over to him, her knees sinking into the duvet. She waited, listening keenly to the tearing of the wrapper and the soft click of the bottle. His hand smoothed over her back and down between her legs. The coolness of the lubrication gave her goose bumps, but his fingers were there, spreading it over and into her as his other hand toyed at her clit. She rested her head on her bent arms, arching up towards him.

Sera felt him press between her buttocks and he was inside her in a smooth, practised stroke. Her breath caught in her throat. She trembled as he held her down with one hand and pressed her clit in small hard circles with the other, timing his thrusts to his hardest strokes on her clit. She gave a small moan and suddenly she was pulled upright against him, his hand in her hair once more. Her scalp ached, but if it meant she was in his arms, the pain didn't matter.

Marc's touch on her clit ceased and she could hardly bear the loss. He thrust into her deeply, pulling her back against his hips. His breathing began to quicken.

"Please, Marc," she begged. She didn't care if she sounded pathetic. She needed it. She needed him.

"No." His thrusts grew rougher and her wetness dripped down her thighs. She was desperate. She leaned her head back against his shoulder and their eyes met. She put all her wanting into her gaze and heard him say "Oui" just before he crushed his lips against hers, rolling her clit between his fingers. He swallowed her cry as she came hard. He thrust into her one last time and she felt him shudder against her.

He pulled out of her and she collapsed into a heap on the bed, euphoric and dazed. She barely registered him shifting her until she was under the covers, tucked up against him in a cocoon of warmth.

"You can still make it six months."

As what he said penetrated the layers of bliss, she shivered.

"No."

"Truly?" He sounded surprised and disappointed. She lifted her head.

"You won't win."

"You underestimate me." Marc wasn't the least bit concerned. It was Sera's turn to chuckle.

"You underestimate Sophie. I would never have made the wager if I thought otherwise."

"Why do you need the money so badly?" She lowered her head back to the pillow. The silence between them stretched uncomfortably.

"You'll have to tell me eventually." Marc reached over and turned off the lamp. Sera closed her eyes, but a hand sliding between her legs made her realize that he wasn't anywhere near finished with her.

Read on for an excerpt from **THE CHRISTMAS GAME**, the third book in the Le Chat Rouge series, to be released in December 2013, and available in ebook.

No calls.

Not a one.

Marc slipped his phone back into the inner pocket of his suit jacket and sat back in the black London taxicab. Sera rarely called him now; their relationship, such as it was, had deteriorated to this. But he would be back in Paris for Christmas, and he didn't want to spend it alone. He'd hoped she would return his call, at least this once.

The cab idled in the heavy traffic of the early evening, the chill rain lashing its windows. Marc glanced outside. They had nearly reached Charing Cross Road, but in this traffic it would be another fifteen minutes before they could make the turn. The red double-decker bus ahead of them inched forward. He buttoned his trench coat and took his umbrella from his bag. Even if he had a broken leg, he could walk faster than this traffic.

"I'll get out here," he told the driver, handing him enough for the fare, plus a generous tip.

"Stay dry." The cabbie laughed at his own joke.

Easier said than done. By the time he reached the sidewalk and could raise his umbrella, he was thoroughly damp and just about chilled through. He walked briskly to the intersection and waited for the light to change. When it did, he crossed over Oxford Street and cut down Soho Street and across the square. The rain seemed to ease as he reached the glass doors of the bookshop on Charing Cross Road, and he took down his umbrella, shaking the rain from the nylon before he closed it up completely.

A clerk greeted him as he entered and he returned her smile. Pretty, with her short, pixie-blonde hair, but far too young.

Barely old enough to vote. He turned his attention to the books, what he'd come for.

The first floor held fiction, and though Marc was famished and ready to go back to Claridge's for supper, he took his time among the shelves. An English bookshop this size didn't exist in Paris and he didn't intend to pass up this opportunity. But though the shop seemed to have miles of shelves, he couldn't find anything to his taste. He was impatient, particular, and the damp had crept down his collar and soaked through the seams of his black brogues and into his socks.

He found the stairs to the upper floors, noting the white A4 taped to the elevator door: Out of Order. An older man squeezed past him, wearing tweed and a navy raincoat. He went up to the next floor and turned a corner, finding the shelves of French novels and books in translation. Much better. He skimmed the titles, but still nothing appealed. A pink-printed spine caught his eye and he pulled it out. Histoire d'O.

The cover was sensual; a woman's bound wrists in black and white, a teasing glimpse of flesh. It reminded him of Sera, her slender body, the last time they'd been together, the silver handcuffs securing her wrists. He put the book back on the shelf, then paused, his hand still on the volume. It could be her Christmas gift. Decided, he continued on, the book in hand. He had one more stop before he could go back to the hotel.

He went up another floor to the Art section, one he knew well. Aside from a specialist bookshop, this was as diverse as he would get. A new art criticism text had been published recently by one of those obscure university presses, a book Sera would roll her eyes at and declare fit for putting her to sleep, and he hoped they had a copy. Keeping up on current academic work helped his business. No one wanted an art dealer who thought Pop Art was the newest thing.

A search of the section brought up nothing. Marc sighed and looked at his watch. He'd have to order it when he got back to Paris. He walked through the aisles, intent on going back to the hotel. When he turned a corner, he came upon a young woman standing on the top step of a gently listing stepladder, reaching up to shelve a small stack of books, one after the other. A Santa hat perched on her head and her ginger hair fell in softly curling waves down her back, and her slim-fitting black uniform trousers high-lighted her curves. He could wait a minute or two.

Madelaine stretched up to place a book on the shelf, push-ing a stray lock of hair from her eyes. The stepladder wobbled un-derneath her but stayed put. The final book, a weighty historical trade paperback, had to be shelved slightly further along, but she didn't want to shift the stepladder that few inches further. She'd just stretch as far as she could manage, and then she'd be done.

Too late.

The stepladder tilted precariously and she felt herself slid-ing forward. The hat fell from her head. She tensed, knowing it was going to hurt. The book slipped off the shelf and hit the floor with a thump.

A strong hand caught her waist, bracing her, and her world tilted upright once more. Madelaine let out a breath of relief, grasping at the shelves in front of her. The hand stayed at her waist and she glanced over her shoulder. Her words of gratitude died on her lips as she came face to face with the most intense dark blue eyes she'd ever seen.

"All right?"

For a moment, she was speechless. The French-accented English washed over her and her cheeks warmed. Of course she couldn't meet a man like him when she was dressed to the nines and out at a club; it had to be when she was in her unflattering work uniform and making a clumsy fool of herself.

"Yes, thank you." She managed a smile, and he stepped back to give her space to climb down to the floor, though she left her hat where it lay on a lower shelf. Hideous thing. He picked up the book from where it had fallen and smoothed out the crumpled pages, reaching up to place it on the shelf. While he did that, show-ing the glint of silver cufflinks at his wrists, his damp trench coat falling open to display his well-cut dark suit and tie, she drank him in. His blue eyes had dark brows to go with them, as well as a strong jaw and a nose that was almost too perfectly straight. He was smiling faintly, but unlike most of the men she'd known, there was no arrogance. Instead, his body language evinced a confidence and surety, a casual ease that most of the investment banker types in central London could learn from. When his attention returned to her, she didn't shy away. He probably had women looking at him all the time anyway.

"De rien," he said, retrieving a book from where it rested on a nearby shelf. Histoire d'O. The corner of her mouth quirked up.

"You came to London to buy a book in French?" she re-marked, stifling the giggle that welled up in her throat.

"It was an impulse."

"Your impulses have good taste."

His gaze caught hers; his stance changed and he seemed to look at her with new interest. "I'm glad you approve. I also came to find another book, but I've had no luck."

"I'd be happy to check for you."

"I'd hoped you would." He followed her to the nearest computer terminal.

"What's the title?" she asked, keying in her information. He recited it for her, giving her the author's name, something Eastern European with more consonants than seemed reasonable, spelling it when her fingers paused on the keys.

One copy. Supposedly. She wasn't familiar with the book, but for this man, she'd find it. Perhaps then he'd forget about her clumsiness.

"You're lucky today." She saw the corner of his mouth turn up and bit back her own smile. "We do have one copy. I didn't think we would, but sometimes this place still surprises me. I didn't think anyone actually read books on art criticism. They're meant to impress, aren't they?"

"I must be one of the few," he quipped. "Are you impressed?"

"Only if you actually read it," she replied, leading him over to the Art section. He chuckled.

"I'll read it. Is art criticism not to your taste?"

"I prefer philosophy, when I'm not reading fiction."

"Really? Any philosopher in particular?"

Madelaine scanned the shelves. "Several. You know, you're probably the art equivalent of me going in and asking for a copy of Sartre's 'Les jeux sont faites'." She shook her head. "Not that I'd be able to find it in English, since it's long out of print."

"I'm not very fond of Sartre, with the exception of some of his plays."

Madelaine glanced to the book he held. "At least you have good taste in erotica."

"Bien sûr. Though this will be a gift for a petite amie."

Lucky woman. He didn't wear a wedding ring, but any man who would buy a copy of The Story of O for a woman was obviously spoken for.

"It's a good book, but parts of it I always found silly."

"Which parts?"

"A chateau? Really? And loads of women willing to service Sir Stephen? As if." Madelaine rolled her eyes. The man chuckled.

"But the prose is good, and it has some other redeeming qualities. It's quite the fantasy."

"I'm sure your girlfriend will love it."

A shadow passed over his face. "Ex, I'm afraid. But she might like it all the same."

"Sorry." An awkward silence descended and Madelaine returned to her search, though inside her heart thrilled at the news. "We do have the book. I wonder if it's been mis-shelved."

"Finding it would be a needle in a haystack, if that's the case." The man's good humour returned. "Unfortunately I can't stay while you look. I need to get back to my hotel."

Madelaine's thrill subsided. Of course. He'd be heading home soon, too. "If you want to leave your information, I could keep searching. Unless you won't be in town?"

"I'll be here until the day after tomorrow," the man said, pulling out his wallet. He extracted a business card and then took a pen from the inside pocket of his suit, turning the card over and writing a number on the back. He gave it to her and she glanced at it.

MARC PERRON

PERRON & FILS, ART DEALERS

There was a Paris address and phone number. Naturally. As if she'd ever be able to look him up in Paris. She could hardly afford to leave the city. "Where are you staying?"

"Claridge's. If you do find the book, let me know. I'd pay to have it delivered to me before I leave." Mr. Perron began to button his trench coat. "I appreciate your help,…?"

"Madelaine," she supplied. He held out his hand and she took it, expecting him to shake her hand. Instead, he brought it to his lips, a move she'd thought cheesy when she'd seen it in films. Except here, now, it sent shivers down her spine.

"Enchantée," he said, letting her hand go almost reluctantly. "I hope to see you again, mademoiselle." His gaze met hers and she saw the desire there, the invitation, should she choose to accept it. But she couldn't, not tonight. She worked until close, and had to be up early to open, thanks to a sick colleague.

"I hope so too," she replied, feeling the embossed letters of his business card under her fingers.

"Trés bien. À demain." She watched him go, and as he reached the stairs, he glanced back at her, the hint of a smile on his lips as he caught her staring. When she didn't break her gaze, he winked at her and mouthed, "Don't forget your hat." Then she did giggle, and saw him laugh.

She had to find that book.

THE LE CHAT ROUGE SERIES

Take a walk on the darker side of Paris...

A jazz club on the Left Bank, Le Chat Rouge seems stuck in another era. Neglect and crime have left their mark, but the club is a haven for the desperate. Sometimes a singer whose talent is worthy of the world's greatest stages, or a patron who has wealth to spare, find their way to its smoky interior.

Gangsters, drug dealers, con artists...many occupy Le Chat Rouge's worn velvet banquettes and tread its creaking parquet floors, but all submit to Royale. The ruthless owner demands loyalty and few earn his favour. Those who do are as brutal as he is, and those who defy him might very well risk their lives.

It's a dangerous place, but fortune awaits the most daring.

ABOUT THE AUTHOR

Alyssa Linn Palmer is a Canadian writer and freelance editor. She splits her time between a full-time day job, and her part-time loves, writing and editing. She is a member of the RWA, the Calgary RWA, and RRW (Rainbow Romance Writers). She has a passion for Paris and all things French, which is reflected in her writing. When she's not writing lesbian romance, she's creating the dark, morally flawed characters of the LE CHAT ROUGE series and indulging in her addictions to classic pulp fiction. You can find her online at www.alyssalinnpalmer.com, or on Twitter @alyslinn.